"We'll have to talk about our future at Weemawee High," said Lauren. "When I was out there on the field, I relived all the bad moments of my life. Like when I had my consultation with the orthodontist and he looked at me solemnly and said, 'Braces!' "

"What does that have to do with our future at Weemawee?" said Patty.

"Well, when I think of something depressing, I immediately try to think of something that's the opposite. Braces are depressing, and popularity is the exact opposite of braces."

"It *is*?"

"It is when you wear braces. So anyway, out there on the football field I thought about how very popular you and I are going to be at Weemawee. This school is going to *appreciate* Patty Greene and Lauren Hutchinson!"

"It *is*? *How*?"

"Haven't the vaguest idea," said Lauren as they walked into the showers.

MARJORIE SHARMAT was born and raised in Portland, Maine, and now lives with her husband in Tucson, Arizona. She is the author of *I Saw Him First,* available in a Dell Laurel-Leaf edition.

SQUARE PEGS™

NOVELIZATION BY
MARJORIE SHARMAT

BASED ON THE EMBASSY TELEVISION
SERIES CREATED BY
ANNE BEATTS

BASED ON THE TELEPLAYS "SQUARE PIGSKINS" BY
ANDY BOROWITZ

"A CAFETERIA LINE" BY
JANIS HIRSCH

AND "THE STEPANOWICZ PAPERS" BY
SUSAN SILVER

LAUREL-LEAF BOOKS bring together under a single imprint outstanding works of fiction and nonfiction particularly suitable
for young adult readers, both in and out of the classroom.
Charles F. Reasoner, Professor Emeritus of Children's Litera-
ture and Reading, New York University, is consultant to this
series.

Published by
Dell Publishing Co., Inc.
1 Dag Hammarskjold Plaza
New York, New York 10017

Laurel-Leaf Library ® TM 766734. Dell Publishing Co., Inc.
ISBN: 0-440-97984-6
RL: 6.0
Printed in the United States of America

First printing—November 1982
Second printing—January 1983

Book Club Edition

1

"On a scale from zero to minus ten, how would you rate our first month at Weemawee High?"

Patty Greene was talking to her best friend, Lauren Hutchinson, as they walked down the halls of Weemawee.

"I'll give it a minus nine," said Lauren. "I used to think that being overweight—*slightly* overweight—and wearing braces were my major obstacles to popularity. But this school is full of obstacles."

"But what if you were me?" said Patty. "What if you were underweight, wore glasses, were younger than your classmates—"

"And smarter," said Lauren. "Don't forget smarter. Because you are."

"But you always say it's social suicide to be smarter," said Patty.

"Maybe it's suicidal just to attend this school," said Lauren.

"I know what you mean. Weemawee could stand some improvement."

"Let me count the ways," said Lauren.

"Start at the top," said Patty, "with Principal Dingleman. He manages to make 'Good morning' sound like a cliché."

5

"And our homeroom teacher, *Ms.* Loomis, keeps telling me what my rights as a woman are while she looms above me. I hate being loomed over. Of course, everybody looms over me, except Marshall Blechtman."

"Marshall's the only person I've ever met who's addicted to white socks because they always match," said Patty. "There's a fascinating mind at work there."

"Not nearly as fascinating as Johnny Slash's. Why would anyone change his name from John Ulasewicz to Johnny Slash? Don't tell me. I know. Otherwise, he couldn't call his car a Slashmobile."

"Right. Ulasewiczmobile just doesn't have the same ring to it."

Patty and Lauren walked toward their lockers. "Things could be worse, I guess," said Lauren. "Muffy Tepperman is our class president."

"What could be worse than that?" asked Patty.

"She could be *running* for class president," said Lauren. "We could drown in a sea of Muffy buttons and be assaulted on every wall by Muffy posters."

"I see a poster face down the hall," said Patty. "And it belongs to Vinnie Pasetta. Dark hair, perfect teeth. He could run for and get elected King of the World."

"Only if Jennifer DiNuccio lets him," said Lauren.

"Oh, Jennifer," said Patty. "It isn't fair that she's so popular, so . . ."

"Say it," said Lauren. "Get it out."

"Pretty."

"Go on."

"That's it."

"There's more. How about pretty . . . stupid? As Jennifer would say, 'Like, you know, I mean, *dumb*!'"

"Well, she has Vinnie as her exclusive property and . . . hey, slow down. Here's *my* exclusive property, humble as it is."

Patty stopped in front of locker 198. She turned the handle of the locker door. The door didn't open. She jiggled the handle. Then she pushed and pulled it.

"It won't open," said Patty. "And I need my books in there for the next class."

"Locker doors never work the first month of school, girl," said a voice in back of her. It was LaDonna Fredericks. "You need help."

"Do you know where the janitor is?" asked Patty.

"As a future show biz celebrity and successor to Diana Ross and Dionne Warwick and various others of tremendous talent, I'm afraid I'm not into janitors," said LaDonna, and she walked on.

"Nuts!" said Patty.

"Accurate description," said Lauren as she pointed to Marshall Blechtman and Johnny Slash, who were coming toward them.

"Maybe they can help," said Patty.

"Yeah, Johnny Slash can summon help from that other world his head resides in," said Lauren.

Patty jiggled the handle again.

"Salutations of the day, ladies," said Marshall. "Marshall Blechtman and Johnny Slash here in person to greet you in front of the grand opening of locker number one ninety-eight. Door prizes—get it? *door* prizes—will be given away hourly. In response to millions of requests, Johnny Slash, the only genuine punk in Weemawee, will perform the Open Your Locker Door Jiggle, guaranteed to win him additional legions of adoring fans."

Johnny Slash lifted his sunglasses, stared into

space, lowered his sunglasses, and said, "I keep telling you, Marshall, I'm not punk, I'm new wave. *Totally* different head. *Totally*." He wobbled his head.

"Thank you, thank you, Johnny Slash," said Marshall. "Autograph seekers, don't push!"

The bell rang. "We're being summoned," said Marshall, "to the Oscars. Best Performance Before a Locker Door."

Johnny Slash picked up Marshall.

"Don't do that!" said Marshall. "It makes me look smaller than I am. It's a misleading act. It's an optical illusion that I, Marshall Blechtman, can easily be lifted off the floor."

Johnny carried Marshall off.

They almost bumped into Muffy Tepperman, who was marching down the hall.

"Hi, guys!" said Muffy. She raised and lowered her eyebrows, contorted her cheeks, and opened and closed her mouth all at the same time.

"She's got the only choreographed face in school," Lauren said to Patty. "Enough moving parts for a chorus line."

Muffy walked up to them. She smoothed her necktie.

"People," she said, "it is my duty to inform both of you that I'm chairperson of the Loitering Committee."

"There's a committee for loitering?" said Lauren. "Great! I always thought that loitering should be organized instead of just happening."

"If you leave these things to chance, they could just fade away and die. I'd hate to see that happen to a wonderful pastime like loitering," Patty added.

"The committee is *against* loitering," said Muffy. "Actually it's just now being formed under my auspices. You see, Weemawee High School must maintain and somewhat upgrade its image, and the very *worst* thing a high school can have, the most *onerous luggage*, you might say, that a school has to carry around is its loiterers. They are like a blotch on the halls of academe."

"Yeah, well, I think there are ointments for that," said Lauren.

"Really!" said Muffy as she walked away. "I'm simply trying to upgrade the already phenomenally high standards of Weemawee High."

"I think she could upgrade the school simply by leaving it," said Patty.

"Leaving the school sounds like a great idea to me," said Lauren. "Like right now. Here comes the *principal*!"

"Hello girls. I'm Winthrop Dingleman, your principal, whose door is always open."

"I wish mine were," said Patty, jiggling her door again.

"Locker trouble?" said Winthrop Dingleman. "We can't have closed doors in this school. I'll send the janitor right up."

He rushed off.

"Help at last," said Patty. "Stay with me until the janitor comes up."

"Okay," said Lauren. "Meanwhile, we can talk. I've looked over the situation at Weemawee High School for us. What I figure we need is a *plan* for getting popular. All really important goals in life are accomplished by detailed plans."

"I guess," said Patty. "You mean, like the Russians' five-year plan? For grain production and stuff?"

Lauren clicked the braces on her teeth. "If it takes

us five *years* to get popular in high school, we'll miss
our first year of *college*! This is a simpler plan. Three
rules for starters. Here, I've made a list."

Patty looked at the list. Then she read it.

" 'Rule One. Stay in close proximity to Jennifer
and her friends at all times.' I don't know, Lauren."

"Patty, listen. Like we'll walk behind them on the
way home every day. Eventually they'll be forced to
ask us to join them."

"Or put attack dogs on us," said Patty.

"Read on," said Lauren.

"Okay. 'Rule Two. Avoid Marshall and Johnny as
much as possible.' That's a good one. 'Rule Three.
Date only highly desirables.' What's a 'highly desirable'?"

Lauren looked discouraged. "Prince Andrew of
England."

"I don't know," said Patty, yawning. "He's not
even next in line for the throne anymore."

"This is serious," said Lauren. "If we really concentrate, we can make it work. Let's swear a secret
oath."

"Okay," said Patty, "but I'm not going to prick my
finger."

"Don't be so immature. That was in junior high,"
said Lauren. "We'll shake hands on this."

Lauren stuck out her hand. "Don't let go of my
hand," she said. "Here comes a *definite* undesirable if
I ever saw one. Wayne Feiger. I can't stand guys you
can *hear* coming."

Wayne Feiger was walking toward Patty and
Lauren. He was carrying a briefcase. Dozens of keys
jingled from his belt. Wayne was the student in charge
of audiovisual showings at school.

Wayne smiled at Patty. Patty continued to try to open her locker. Wayne just stood there.

"Hi, Wayne," said Patty.

"Hi, Patty," said Wayne. He stared at her blankly. He moved slightly. Dozens of keys jingled.

At last Patty said, "I enjoyed the movie you showed in assembly last week."

"Yeah?" Wayne paused. "Well, thanks, but I don't make 'em. I only run 'em."

There was another long, long pause. Patty banged on her locker; it still wouldn't open. Then Lauren banged on it. But nothing happened.

Wayne shifted his feet. He jingled. Finally he said to Patty, "I was wondering if you might possibly be free after school for a Coke, but you're probably not."

"Today?" said Patty. "Well, as a matter of fact, I'm—"

Lauren hit her in the ribs. "Going shopping with me," said Lauren. "Remember?"

"Oh, right," said Patty. "I'm sorry, Wayne."

"It's okay," said Wayne. "I didn't think you'd go, but my mother always says ask anyway . . . it can't hurt."

Wayne walked off, jingling. The clinking sounded mournful to Patty. She glared at Lauren. "Why did you make me do that?"

"Remember the plan? He's a *total* creep."

"Yeah, but *my* mother always says go out with everyone who asks you, *even* a creep, because maybe you'll meet someone else."

"Sure . . . another creep. Come on, we're going to be late. Almost everyone's in class."

"But the janitor is supposed to be right up," said Patty.

"To someone as old as Mr. Stepanowicz, 'right up' could mean next Thursday," said Lauren.

Suddenly Lauren spotted something, "Don't look!" she said.

Patty immediately turned to look.

"I said don't look!"

Patty turned back.

"Okay, *now* look," said Lauren.

Patty turned again. There was the handsomest guy she had ever seen. He was taking a drink from the fountain. He was tall and blond and was wearing a tight white T-shirt and janitor's overalls on his gorgeous body.

He headed toward them.

"He's dazzling!" said Patty. "Tell me how long I can look before going blind."

The blond guy walked up to Patty. "Patty Greene?" he asked. "Locker one ninety-eight."

"Yes! That's me! What do I win! I mean, yes?"

"Hi. So what's wrong with your locker?"

"Huh? Oh . . . someone's getting Mr. Stepanowicz. It's okay, I mean . . . he'll be right up."

"He is. *I'm* Stepanowicz . . . only you can call me Steve."

Steve smiled. It was a great smile.

"You're the—the . . ." Patty began.

Lauren was shaking her head violently behind Steve's back and grimacing no!

Patty finished. "Maintenance engineer?"

Steve seemed to like the sound of that. Lauren nodded behind his back and made an okay sign to Patty.

"Yeah," said Steve, "I guess you could call it that. Yeah. Temporary. My old man had a heart attack, and I'm helping out till he gets back."

"Oh, good. I mean . . . I'm sorry for your dad," said Patty. "I hope he'll be all right."

"Yeah, me, too. If I had to spend my days cooped up inside like this, I'd flip out. I live up north, in the woods, *alone*!"

Steve stood in front of the locker. "Let's see what we've got here." He smiled another great smile. At Lauren. "Excuse me, hon." Lauren was reluctant to move an inch from him.

Just then a bell went off, signaling class. Lauren continued to watch Steve. He had several tools with him, but he looked the locker over and gave it a little jam with his elbow. The locker door flew open.

He grinned his great grin once again. "There you go. Next time you have a problem, give it a little elbow, or if you want, call me. Take care, girls."

"Oh, sure, thanks. Thanks," said Patty. "Bye."

Steve turned and winked at Lauren. She felt her knees go wobbly.

Patty grabbed her books out of the locker and closed it carefully. "Come on," she said to Lauren, "we really are late now."

Patty started to run to class. Then she stopped and turned. She realized that Lauren wasn't with her.

Lauren was leaning against the locker, touching it where Steve had elbowed it. She looked as if she were in a daze.

Patty rushed back. "What's wrong?" she asked.

"He called me hon! Did you see his hair, his muscles, his smile, his *muscles*?"

"You said that twice."

"They deserve repeating. Once for *each* bicep. I'm definitely in love!"

Patty and Lauren were washing their hands in the washroom.

"You can't be in love with Steve," said Patty.

"Why not? He said he lives alone. He's not married."

"You hate the woods."

"Did you see his smile! His dimple—I'm in love!"

Patty dried her hands. "You don't even know him," she said. "He's way too old, and he's—he's"— she leaned over and whispered—"a janitor."

"Maintenance engineer. And temporary!"

"But your mother'll kill you. She wants you to marry a doctor."

"You know what a clean freak my mother is. I was ten before I realized that Lemon Pledge wasn't her *perfume*. She'd love having someone in the family she could discuss acrylic floor covering with."

Lauren started to shake her hands dry.

"But this could be worse than living with your mother if he made you clean up your room *all* the time," said Patty.

"I'm sure he won't 'bring the basement home with him,' " Lauren said.

"Besides, what about our plan?" asked Patty. "I mean, *he's* not exactly royalty. You wouldn't let me go out with Wayne Feiger and you're going to date a janitor? That's all Jennifer has to hear . . . and you can forget being popular with anyone other than people who read *Popular Mechanics*. And you know how popular they are!"

Lauren walked toward the washroom door. "If you don't want to stand by me, I don't care. I'll go alone. I must go where my heart leads me."

"Where?"

"To the basement."

"To the basement?" Patty scratched her head.

Two minutes later Patty and Lauren were stealthily walking toward a cagelike room which had a sign, "JANITORIAL AREA."

"You're going to get in trouble," said Patty.

"Oh, I hope so," said Lauren.

Slowly they walked toward the cage. They kept turning to make certain that no one was around.

"What if someone sees us?" asked Patty.

"We'll tell them we're just learning the school," said Lauren. "Like in a hotel? You're supposed to familiarize yourself with escape routes for fires."

"That's when you're on the fiftieth floor. We're in the *basement*."

"Okay, so we'll tell them this is just in case of a nuclear holocaust."

"Here we are," said Patty. She peered inside the cage.

"Let's go inside," said Lauren.

"Let's not," said Patty.

"Oh, c'mon," said Lauren, and she walked inside. Patty followed her.

"It's empty," said Lauren. "But at least I can touch everything. Look, this is his jacket. This is his saw." She ran her hands over the saw lovingly. "This is—"

"Crazy," said Patty. "This is truly crazy."

"Why? When you were in love with Danny Zipser, you carried the pink eraser he gave you everywhere you went. You slept with it under your pillow."

"We were also eight at the time," said Patty. "And the only harm *that* did was possibly confuse the tooth fairy."

"Well, I want something of Steve's to keep. These are his wood shavings."

"I don't think they'll fit into a locket. I'd hold out for a piece of his hair if I were you," said Patty.

The bell rang.

"Let's go," said Patty, and she pulled Lauren out.

"Wait! I have to go back," said Lauren.

Lauren went back into the cage, grabbed some wood shavings, and ran out.

Patty telephoned Lauren. "Lauren, how firm are we on Rule Three of our plan?"

"Firm. Very firm."

"But what about Steve, the, uh, temporary maintenance engineer?"

"We've been over this, Patty. In my opinion he's highly desirable. He qualifies for our plan."

"Well, would you reconsider Wayne Feiger?" asked Patty.

"I wouldn't even consider him," said Lauren. "Why?"

"Well, his mother told him that it wouldn't hurt to ask me out again. So that's what he just did. He called me up."

"And you turned him down, of course?"

"Well, not outright."

"What does 'not outright' mean?"

"I accepted him."

"You *what*?"

"Lauren, he was just minding his mother. It was kind of sad."

"Minding his mother? He's in high school. Does she still tell him to look both ways before he crosses the street? 'Oh, Wayne, you must eat every drop of your strained spinach or you can't have dessert.' "

"Lauren!"

"Look, he listens to his mommy. You listen to me. Call him back and break the date."

"I can't."

"Why not?"

"He's on his way over. The date is for right now. This afternoon."

"You're ruined. You're absolutely ruined. Being seen with Wayne Feiger is like admitting that you're hard up."

"I *am* hard up."

"But you don't advertise it. You don't *jingle* it. I suppose he's showing up with his entire family of keys."

"I didn't ask."

"Look, I'll hang up right now! Call his house just in case he hasn't left. Break the date."

"But—"

"What if Jennifer and Vinnie see you out with Wayne?"

"Hang up fast!" said Patty.

Lauren hung up. Patty quickly looked up Wayne Feiger's number in the telephone book. She dialed it.

"Hello."

It was his mother!

"Hello, is Wayne there, please?"

"Who is it who's calling and wants to know? A name, please."

"Patty Greene."

"You're his three thirty date, aren't you?"

"Well, that's what I'm calling about," said Patty.

"You're extremely fortunate to be going out with my Wayne," said his mother.

"Well . . ."

"He could have had others."

"Yes, well . . ."

"Sometimes they line up outside the front door."

"They *do*?"

"You'd better believe it, young lady. What is it about you that makes you the lucky one this afternoon?"

"Uh . . ."

"Personality? Is it personality? I've never met you, so I can't comment on your outward appearance. At this moment all I can do is assess your personality and, of course, poise. You seem to be lacking in poise. Too many 'wells, uhs,' and the like. My Wayne is usually attracted to positive personalities."

"Well, then maybe I'm not right for him," said Patty.

"That's for Wayne to decide. Even if I don't think you're suited to each other, it's not my decision to make. I believe in being a hands-off mother. Interfering mothers simply mess up their children's lives."

"I know."

"Well, this conversation has been most enjoyable. But I'll let you go so you can get ready for Wayne. By the way, he doesn't like girls who put too much gunk on their faces. Just a little tip."

"Uh, I was wondering if he's there. I wanted to talk to him about this afternoon."

"He was here when you called, but he left while you were talking to me. By the way, another tip, Wayne doesn't go for heavy talkers. If you cool it just a tiny bit, you'll have a better chance to impress him. Don't tell him I said so. He might think we're in *cahoots*!"

"I won't tell him."

"Clever. I'm looking forward to meeting you."

"Right."

"Say, in about an hour?"

"An hour?"

"Wayne always brings his girls home for my approval. It's a kind of predate plan. I don't encourage it, but I do think it's touching. None of his friends bring their dates home to their mothers. Alienation. That's what I call it. Well, see you in sixty."

"All right. Bye."

"Wait! Wayne likes green. He adores green."

"I'll remember. Bye."

"See you in sixty."

Patty went to her closet. She changed from the green sweater she was wearing to a bright blue one.

"Forgive me, Lauren," she said. "A plan is a sacred thing. It should never be tampered with."

The doorbell rang. Patty sighed. If only motherhood were a passing fad.

4

Vinnie Pasetta was sitting on the steps with some of his friends when Patty and Lauren walked by.

"Yo, Patty," said Vinnie.

"Me?" Patty couldn't believe he was yoing *her*!

"You see any other Pattys around? So, could I ask you something?"

"Anything," said Patty as she whipped off her glasses and tried to hide them. Oh, why couldn't she be cool in front of Vinnie?

"It's like kinda personal," said Vinnie.

Lauren was standing there, watching. Patty made a motion for her to leave. She hoped Vinnie didn't notice it.

"Oh. Right," said Lauren. "Excuse me . . . I'll just . . . uh . . . tie my shoe."

Patty whispered to her, "You're wearing *loafers*. Next time just say you have to comb your hair. Hair is always safe."

Lauren walked off.

Vinnie said, "You suppose I could cheat off you on the history test Monday? I mean, you getting straight A's and all."

Patty hoped her disappointment didn't show. "Uh, sorry, Vinnie . . . I don't cheat."

"Yeah, well, you don't *have* to. I mean, I'm the one who does the cheating. You just *let* me."

Patty was thinking. She *wanted* to help Vinnie. Possibly, if he asked her, she would scrub floors for him. She would definitely jump from a helicopter for him. Shielding him from a charging bull was another possibility. But helping him cheat! No. She had some standards. Even if he *was* a fox and she—she . . . wasn't. She put her glasses back on.

"No . . . I'm sorry," she said. "I don't *believe* in cheating. But I could help you study—if you want."

"No, thanks. I don't believe in *studying*. Unless it's with Jennifer, and that's not history . . . it's *biology*."

Just then Jennifer came up and glared at Vinnie and Patty. "Okay, Vincent, like, if you had a mind, there'd be just one thing on it."

Maybe she'll give him a kibble if he runs after her fast enough, Patty sighed.

Patty caught up with Lauren. Lauren didn't even notice her. She was looking down at a folder she was carrying.

"Lauren, hurry up," said Patty. "Let's start part one of our plan . . . walking behind Jennifer and her friends and listening!"

Patty rushed off behind Jennifer and Vinnie.

Lauren looked up from her folder. "Patty, were you here? Where did you go?"

Lauren ran into the building after Patty. She rounded a corner quickly. She didn't see the wet floor or the mop or the bucket. She started to fall. She felt a strong arm reach out to steady her.

"Steve!"

Steve caught her as she was about to fall. She looked up into his face. There was his great grin again. She couldn't speak.

"Take it easy," said Steve. "Whoever he is, he'll wait."

"Oh, no, I . . . thanks . . . oh . . ."

Lauren looked down at the floor and saw that it was all wet. "I'm sorry . . . I spoiled your . . . floor." She started to walk. "I'll just try to walk on the dry spots, wherever they may be. Oh, dear, I'm stuck on a little dry island, with water, water everywhere."

Steve laughed. He came over and lifted her to the dry spot on the other side.

"Oh, you didn't have to do that . . . I must be heavy. . . ."

Lauren was angry at herself for not going on the crash diet she'd read about in a magazine. It would have been worth restricting herself to artichokes and sardines for this one precious moment when Steve would have felt he was carrying a slender nymphet over the waters of Weemawee.

"Light as a feather," said Steve, and he walked away.

Lauren was in shock. She turned, took one step, slipped, and fell. She was afraid to look up. What if he had seen her fall. *Her*, the *feather*!

But he was gone.

Lauren started to get up. She saw Jennifer standing against a door. *Jennifer* had seen her fall.

"Like, those dance lessons you took really paid off," said Jennifer.

Jennifer flounced by.

Even she can't bother me today, thought Lauren. *Even my braces don't bother me. Even the prospect of going on a crash diet to make myself even more feathery and light. Even the fact that I'm now sounding like Betty Crocker and Duncan Hines doesn't bother me. I'm walking on air. Steve lifted me. If I had known when I started out for school today that I'd be lifted . . . well, Weemawee High, you're my kind of school.*

5

Ms. Allison Loomis looked at her blackboard with pride. There was her poster of the heart and all the internal workings—veins, capillaries, ventricles, atria, all the beautiful things that made the heart her favorite part of the body.

She looked across a room of bored faces, doodling hands, and joking students. How could they be so detached when faced with something so important, so pulsing?

"And that finishes our chapter on the heart," she said. "I think we might say that this organ is indeed the heart of the matter, so to speak, in that it is vital to our bodily functions."

The bell rang. Everyone was packing up their books. Lauren walked slowly up to Ms. Loomis.

"Ms. Loomis," she said, "everything we study about the heart is mechanical, like the veins flow *to* and the arteries flow *away*. Well, how come we don't ever talk about the emotional part? Words like 'heart-broken' and 'heartache'—"

Miss Loomis suddenly looked excited. "Yes! Yes! I see what you mean. A very, if I may say, poetic way of looking at this organ. Of course, there *is* nothing we can do about broken hearts, physically, that is."

Ms. Loomis started to think about her own bad experiences with men. For openers, there was her ex-husband. There was no point in thinking about *him*.

Ms. Loomis broke in two the pencil she was holding. "We just must learn to suffer!" she said.

Suddenly the door to the classroom opened. Steve walked in. "You got a broken blind here?"

Ms. Loomis stared at him. Ms. Loomis didn't believe in staring at men. "We're simply aping what men do to us," she often said. Ms. Loomis was astounded at what she was seeing. All this glory assembled in one body. Perhaps if she thought about this man in a classical manner, as a kind of Grecian specimen . . .

Ms. Loomis addressed those few who were still hanging around the room. "However, each day dawns new with the promise of sunshine coming into our lives. Our hearts *can* be full again."

Ms. Loomis went up to Steve and fluttered her eyelashes. She had forgotten that she called this the "ultimate noodlehead gesture." She took him by the hand and led him to the broken blind. "Just follow me," she said. "So you're the new janitor?"

"Maintenance engineer." Steve corrected her with some pride.

Kids were watching and listening. They were hysterical. But Lauren was livid. She turned to Patty. "I've got competition."

"How do you know?"

"Well, if Ms. Loomis were a praying mantis, she'd have *digested* Steve by now!"

"Lauren, it's not a very wise idea to compete with your teacher for a man."

"Why not? It's better than competing with Miss America."

"You have a point," said Patty.

6

Lauren dressed up everyday for school. Each day she tried a little harder. Each day she wore something new. Each day she put something new on her face.

And she watched Steve.

One day he was installing lights in the home ec classroom. He didn't see her. She wrote something down.

The next day she looked out the window as a pickup truck pulled away. She wrote something down.

"I'm in seventh heaven," Lauren said to Patty one day as they sat alone at a table in the cafeteria, surrounded by papers and envelopes. Then she looked around to see if anyone was noticing. "I'm not the only occupant up there. I'm telling you, Ms. Loomis *wants* Steve!"

"Maybe you're imagining things," said Patty. "Is that another new outfit?"

"Naw," said Lauren. "I just never had anyone to wear it for before."

"How do you know you'll even see him? My locker is working perfectly!"

"I know where he is every minute of the day," said Lauren. "Look, I have an entire Stepanowicz file—his route, his schedule. Of course, emergencies, closed drains."

"How did you get *that*?"

"I followed him on his rounds."

Patty looked at the ceiling. "I'm impressed by your self-control." She reached down into the folder and pulled out a pressed flower. "A dried rose?" she said. "He gave you a rose?"

"No . . . but I can pretend he did. For now."

"Lauren, don't you think you're carrying this a little too far. I mean, it's really just a fantasy."

"*So far*. But what's wrong with a fantasy? Fantasy is what makes life livable! Look, I've got a complete file on him. I wrote down everything he said and did." Lauren started to read: " 'Excuse me, hon.' 'Take it easy.' 'Eight seventeen.' 'Light as a feather'—that's my favorite so far.

'Achew'—"

"What's 'achew'?"

"He was watering outside, and he sneezed."

"Did you collect the Kleenex or did he use his sleeve?"

"For someone who's supposed to be my best friend, you're not very supportive," said Lauren. "If you *want* something enough, you can *make* it happen! The mind is a very *powerful* weapon. Oh, no, here come two people whose weapons are definitely *not* loaded!"

"It must be Marshall and Johnny Slash," said Patty without looking up.

"Hi," said Marshall.

"Sorry, guys," said Lauren. "We're kind of busy. With something personal."

"Wait," Patty said to Marshall and Johnny. Then she whispered to Lauren, "I already broke Rule Three, so I'm breaking Rule Two. Besides, we've been ignoring them all week. It's kind of mean."

Patty smiled up at Marshall and Johnny. "You can sit here. Put your trays down."

Lauren quickly gathered up their things and hid them away in her folder. Marshall noticed what she was doing. Johnny, as usual, was in his own world.

"So, ladies and germs," said Marshall, "what's happening?"

"In the real world?" said Patty. "Not much."

"I haven't talked to you for a few days, Lauren," said Marshall. "You're always running downstairs. What are you doing?"

"I'm in training for *Rocky Four*."

Marshall turned to Patty. "What's with her?"

"Nothing," said Patty. "She's got her mind on something else."

"Oh," said Marshall, "I was going to take it personally, but . . . I guess that would be silly. Wouldn't it?"

There was a long pause.

"Wouldn't it?" he repeated.

"Sometimes the truth hurts," said Johnny.

"Then lie," said Marshall.

Lauren ignored him and checked her folder. Then

she whispered to Patty, "I'm going to miss him waxing the gym. I bet I'll see his shoulder blades fully flexed when he pushes the waxer. I'll be back. Guard this folder with your *life*!"

Lauren jumped up and ran out of the cafeteria.

Marshall shrugged. "I'm kind of getting the feeling of being neglected, but I can't put my finger on why."

Johnny took off his sunglasses and spoke to them. "Because Lauren hasn't spoken to you in three days?"

"Yeah," said Marshall. He looked depressed. "What's wrong with her? She's usually kind of rude and stuff, but comedians are used to 'no respect.' Only lately I get the feeling she's totally *forgotten* about me."

"*Totally*," said Johnny.

"It's just a phase," said Patty.

Johnny wobbled his head and spoke into space. "Remember when I was heavily into punk. I came to my senses eventually."

Patty smiled and got up to throw away her empty carton of milk and put away her tray. She left the folder on the table.

Just then LaDonna and Jennifer walked by. Jennifer looked down and noticed the folder. It was marked in red "DO NOT READ!!! BY LAUREN HUTCHINSON."

Jennifer picked it up.

"Hey, like, what's this? 'Do Not Read by Lauren Hutchinson.' 'Top secret.' 'Not For Your Eyes.' Oh, yummy."

LaDonna read, " 'You will be shot.' This *is* heavy."

"Okay, like, it's some kind of secret code, you know?" said Jennifer.

Patty came rushing back. "Hey, what are you doing? Can't you read?"

"Like, what do you think I'm *doing*?" said Jennifer.

She laughed and waved the folder over her head. Things spilled out of it and fell all over the floor. Marshall and Johnny rushed to help Patty gather everything up.

Jennifer yawned and put down the empty folder. "You know, I think that's, like, enough exercise so soon after lunch."

"Is that a rule?" asked Johnny. "Like, not swimming an hour after you eat?"

Marshall gathered up the rest of the papers and other things that were in the folder. "Here, Patty, I think that's all." Marshall started to hand everything to Patty. He looked down at what he was holding. "What is this anyway?"

Patty answered quickly and sharply. "Nothing!"

Johnny spoke up. "It's just top secret, Marshall . . . it's *nothing*!"

Marshall kept looking. "Wait a minute. This is a diagram of the basement of *this* school. This says, 'when *he* fixed the locker.' Lauren is keeping a file on someone named 'he' with little hearts and her name written 'Mr. and Mrs. Stepanowicz'—this is all about the *janitor*?"

Jennifer and LaDonna quickly grabbed some of the papers. Johnny lifted his sunglasses and joined them. Now Marshall, Johnny, Jennifer, and LaDonna all were looking at the contents of Lauren's folder.

Patty frantically tried to gather the papers and put them away. "Stop reading, and hand those over!" she said. She felt desperate. She was supposed to be the guardian of the folder. She couldn't let her best friend down.

"I don't get it," said Jennifer. "Okay, I've heard of Janitor in a Drum—is this, like, you know, Janitor in a Folder?"

Patty finally managed to grab everything and put it away. Marshall sank down in his chair in shock.

"I've lost Lauren to a janitor? Mr. Clean? The man from Glad?"

Johnny tried to be helpful. "The guy in the tidy bowl?"

"My heart is broken," said Marshall.

LaDonna grinned. "Maybe the janitor can fix it. He should be good at that."

Then LaDonna and Jennifer exchanged gleeful slaps. "Like, that was a good one," said Jennifer.

"You have to admit he is a fox," said LaDonna, "even though he is a janitor."

"Yeah, well, *Vinnie* is low enough for *me*," said Jennifer.

Johnny was in intense communication with himself. "Lauren and Mr. Stepanowicz? Wow . . . like, he's kind of old. But well, a May-December romance could work. Of course, he does walk kind of slow and she walks kind of fast, but that's okay. There *is* this height thing that could even out because old people *do shrink* as they get older and she could still *grow* as *she* gets older . . . so yeah, it'll be okay."

As usual, Johnny was very pleased with what he had learned from himself.

But Marshall just sat staring sadly into space.

Suddenly Lauren came running back. She dashed up to Patty. "Give me the book! He said, 'Don't walk there.' "

Lauren reached out for her book. Marshall started to hand her the folder. Johnny handed her the book. LaDonna and Jennifer were laughing and pointing. They pretended they were pushing a mop and did mop-pushing dance steps as they sang, "Mr. Clean, Mr. Clean."

Vinnie walked in. "Vinnie!" Jennifer called. "Lauren's got a crush on the janitor!"

Lauren was stunned. Then she turned to Patty. "You told them!"

Patty had never seen Lauren so furious. Furious at her! "No, I didn't tell them . . ." she began.

"You just gave them my folder? I told you to guard it with your life. They're reading it, and you're still *alive*!"

Lauren grabbed the folder from Marshall's hand and rushed away.

Patty stared after her. If only she hadn't been so careless with her friend's private things! A careless friend was worse than no friend at all.

Jennifer and LaDonna were still singing and dancing around.

"Wash your mouths out!" said Patty. "Preferably with Mr. Clean!"

7

Ms. Allison Loomis tapped her desk with a pointer, trying to get order. "Class, class, stop fanning yourselves! Stop pretending to pass out! Stop talking! Stop laughing!"

"Like, should we, you know, stop breathing?" asked Jennifer.

Ms. Loomis tapped her desk again. Sometimes she thought her class didn't understand the function of a teacher, actually the function of a school. "Learning" was a strange sort of exotic word that they hadn't come to grips with. And now that the temperature control in her room was out of order, her class was completely out of order. "*Totally*," as Johnny Slash observed.

I can rise to this challenge, Ms. Loomis thought. *I can find new inspiration in this heat. I can be a kind of teacher in the tropics, the Albert Schweitzer of Weemawee High.*

She tapped her desk once again. "Class, class, get hold of yourselves."

"Awww, we'd rather get hold of someone else, Miss Loomis," said Vinnie.

"Vincent, you know I request that you address all females as *Ms.*, and I suggest you *start* with *me*."

Vinnie smirked. "My pleasure . . . Ms. Loomis."

The class laughed hysterically.

"Class, I realize that you are all *very*, *very* hot."

The class was now laughing *and* hooting. Ms. Loomis choose to ignore what she was hearing. Did Schweitzer ever get hooted at? She would have to research that.

She continued. "But the temperature control has gone awry."

Ms. Loomis started to pass out papers. "We shall carry on. I suggest we continue with yesterday's quiz on Chapter Two, 'The Body and Its Functions.' "

LaDonna spoke up. "You know, it's very hard to function when your bod's perspiring, Ms. Loomis."

"For sure," said Jennifer. "I mean, I am, like, *really* hot."

Vinnie whistled *awooo*.

Ms. Loomis sighed and then gave a note to a student. "Deliver this immediately," she said. "Don't dawdle. Have respect for the *urgency* of your mission."

"Yeah," said Vinnie. "Respect that urgency. Don't get fresh with it on your first date!"

The student took the note and left.

Johnny Slash spoke up. "It is hot in here, though, Ms. Loomis. How hot is it?"

Johnny turned to Marshall and gestured for Marshall to take over. "Marshall, how hot is it? It's so hot . . ."

But Marshall didn't pick up the comedy cue. He just sat there like a sad ex-comedian. "I can't be funny," he said, "when I'm crying on the inside. Although if I sang, I could do a good Pagliacci like Sergio Franchi does in his nightclub act."

"Like, I love his jeans," said Jennifer. "Like, my make-up wouldn't, you know, streak."

Patty wasn't listening to what was going on. She

was too busy trying to get Lauren's attention. They were sitting side by side, but Lauren had turned her back on Patty. She refused to turn toward her.

"Lauren," Patty whispered, "come on. You don't honestly think I would betray your confidence. Do you?"

"If the shoe fits . . ."

"I just got up for one second—"

Ms. Loomis addressed the class. "I sense a great deal of conversational fragmentation," she said, "inspired, no doubt, by this oppressive heat. But relief is on the way. I have arranged for the janitor to come up."

The class was hooting louder than she had ever heard. She realized that it had been a mistake for her to think she was Albert Schweitzer. She should have chosen a *woman* as her role model. She tried to think of a woman who had battled tremendous heat under adverse conditions. But all that came to mind was the lady on the TV commercial who resourcefully made Kool-Aid for all the neighborhood children.

She didn't know why the students were yelling, "Lauren's lover boy to the rescue." "Top secret." "Hey, Lauren . . ."

Ms. Loomis studied Lauren. Was this her competition? Her eyes locked with Lauren's.

She's fourteen years old and I'm . . . not! thought Ms. Loomis.

Lauren ignored the taunts. She sat up straight, stuck out her chin, and took out her mirror and comb. She fixed her hair.

Ms. Loomis said, "Now I want you all to pass your papers to the person across the aisle to grade. Business as usual. Mr. Pasetta, that means *you.*"

Vinnie, who had been standing up, went back to his seat. Everyone passed papers except Lauren. She refused to give her paper to Patty. She reached across Patty and exchanged with the girl who was sitting on the other side. The girl just shrugged.

Patty said to Lauren, "Please, let me explain."

Lauren looked at her coldly. "No explanation is necessary. Actions speak louder than words, and a fair-feather friend is—"

"That's 'weather,' a fair *weather* friend."

"I close the iron door on you. Tight."

Ms. Loomis spoke. All right, class, the answer to the first question is . . . liver. Hands? How many had liver?"

Some of the students raised their hands.

"I never touch it. Spinach neither," said Vinnie.

Suddenly the door opened. Steve strode in, a glorious presence carrying a toolbox.

The class started to whisper among themselves.

Ms. Loomis raised her arm in greeting. "Hallelujah! Mr. Stepanowicz. Our knight in shining armor." Ms. Loomis turned coy. She looked up at Steve. "Don't tell Gloria Steinem I had to call for your help."

The class broke up in laughter. "We'll keep your secret from Gloria," said Vinnie. "Don't nobody tell *Ms*. Steinem."

"Like, you know, my lips are sealed with gloss," said Jennifer.

Lauren was staring at Steve. He was so wonderful!

Ms. Loomis sidled up to Steve. She, too, was busy staring at him. She had never really thought much about muscles. Until now. Muscles had their place in the universe. She stood right next to Steve as he began to work on the temperature control, which was right next to Lauren's desk. Steve put the control cover on her desk. Lauren fingered it lovingly.

Ms. Loomis was now standing very close to Steve.

"Excuse me," said Steve. "I need the light."

Ms. Loomis jumped back. "Oh, yes, of course. The light." She looked at him coyly. "Well, Doctor, what's your diagnosis?"

"That's funny. Someone stuck this broken pencil in here and jammed this," Steve said. Everyone looked at Ms. Loomis. She was blushing. Steve turned to Lauren. "Hon, could you hand me that cover, please?"

Lauren reached for the cover.

Ms. Loomis reached for the cover.

Lauren won.

Lauren handed the cover to Steve as if it were a holy grail. Their hands touched!

The class went wild. Steve seemed oblivious to what was happening. "There you go," he said. "All fixed. No sweat—that's a joke."

"That's a joke?" said Marshall.

Marshall looked disgusted.

Ms. Loomis was still enthralled. She touched Steve's arm in thanks. She aimed at the muscle. "Thank you *so very, very much*, Steve, for your prompt and *productive* performance."

Steve nodded. Then he picked up his toolbox and left. As he walked out, he waved and smiled at the class.

Lauren felt ecstatic. *He's smiling and waving at* me! she thought. *These throngs of people are as nothing. He cut right through them and aimed at me.* Lauren opened her book and wrote down everything that Steve had done and said.

Patty sat silently. She felt depressed.

"Hey, Ms. Loomis," Vinnie yelled, "maybe you can get him to regulate *your* thermostat after school."

Ms. Loomis glared at Vinnie. She had an I can-flunk-you-in-an-instant look in her eye. Vinnie got busy with his books.

Marshall felt sick. He buried his head in his hands. Then he shook his head from side to side. "Did you hear his timing? He can't even tell a joke!"

Somewhere in the foggy recesses of Johnny Slash's brain a light went on. "Oh, no! The father *and* the son!"

8

After class Lauren walked alone to her locker. She found a mop leaning against it. She grinned. *This must mean* Steve *is near!* she thought. She grabbed the mop eagerly and looked around the hall for a sign of him.

Then she saw Vinnie and his pals. They were cracking up with laughter.

"You planted this here to tease me," said Lauren. "Cute! And very appropriate for a bunch of mopheads like you!"

Lauren held the mop close to her as she headed for the basement. This mop was a blessing in disguise. The perfect excuse to see Steve!

Patty was standing at a distance, watching Lauren walk off with the mop. She shook her head and sighed.

In the basement Lauren bumped into Steve almost immediately. She was on her way in as he was on his way out. Her good luck was piling up today!

"Oh . . . hi," she said. "Uh, somehow this got upstairs, and I thought maybe it was yours. I mean—"

Lauren stumbled over her words. It was so difficult to be sophisticated about a mop.

"I was wondering how that walked away," Steve said. "Thanks. Mind putting it away? I've got a leaky john to get."

Lauren started to say more, but Steve was gone. She lovingly returned the mop to its empty notch in the supply rack. Then she took out her folder and quickly wrote down the details of their latest exchange in her Steve book.

She ran out of paper. She grabbed a piece of sandpaper and continued to write: "I've got a leaky john to get."

What an intimate piece of information to share with a girl, she thought. *Next he'll be confessing* everything.

When Lauren finished writing, she headed for the cafeteria. She found an empty table and sat down by herself. She opened her folder and started to read what she had written. She saw Patty coming toward her with a tray.

Lauren quickly spread her papers all over the table to make sure there was no room for Patty's tray. Patty watched her. She felt hurt, but she didn't say anything.

Patty looked down at the covered table, she looked at Lauren, and then she silently left.

Patty joined Marshall and Johnny, who were just finishing their lunches. Marshall seemed to be in a bad mood. *We can be in a bad mood together,* Patty thought as she put her tray down.

"I just can't believe it," Patty said as she started to eat. "She refuses to speak to me! It's not fair.. . . Maybe it'll just die on its own. I mean, my mother says every girl goes through a rebellious phase—like dating people their parents don't approve of."

"That's it," said Marshall, lighting up with inspiration. "I'll call her mother."

"Good idea," said Johnny.

"Don't you dare!" said Patty.

"On the other hand," said Johnny.

"Why not?" said Marshall. "It's for her own good. I'll do it anonymously." Marshall cleared his throat, changed his expression, and assumed a weird voice. "It's ten o'clock. Do you know where your daughter is? Out with a janitor."

"Marshall!" Patty was annoyed. "That'll only get Lauren in trouble. Is that what you want?"

"Desperate men do desperate things," said Marshall. Then he added, "Well, what else can we do? I mean, look at all the things I can offer her, and she picks some guy for his tools!"

Johnny looked up. He was having a lucid moment. "She's seriously mad at you, Patty, huh?"

Patty felt defensive. "It's not my fault," she said. Then she paused. "Well, I left the table for only one second."

Johnny suddenly remembered the file. "It's all over?" he asked.

Patty sighed. "I guess these things happen between friends."

"Yeah, Marshall," said Johnny, "it's probably like when you and I had that fight about who was taller. Remember? You lost because I could describe the way you part your hair."

9

Lauren was sitting alone in the ladies' room. She was looking in the mirror. *What good does it do to wear your best dress when you have a red spot on your nose and your smile is having an off day?* she asked herself.

Lauren put some makeup on her nose. She checked it out from different angles. She practiced her repertory of smiles. Then she started to rehearse her speech in a soft voice.

" 'Hi Steve . . . I'd like to talk to you for a moment.' No. Uh . . . 'Steve, someone has to take the initiative, and I know you probably think it's not proper to talk to me first, like a doctor can't make a move on a patient, it's unethical.' No—"

Suddenly Lauren jumped. Jennifer had come into

the room. Had she heard? Obviously not. She wore
her regular superior look, not the fiendish look of
superiority that came over her when she had something on someone else.

Lauren spoke. She tried to seem calm. "Hi, you
scared me."

"Good," said Jennifer.

"I mean, not scared me, startled me. I'm a little
nervous."

"Why? Just because of that zit on your nose?"

Lauren immediately covered her nose with her
hand. Then she took it off slowly to see if it really was
that bad. "Does it really show that badly?" she asked.

"Okay," said Jennifer. "The best thing to do is to
put a hot towel on it—that brings it up real fast, you
know."

"Oh, yeah? Thanks," said Lauren. She felt grateful
to Jennifer for sharing this information. And Jennifer
had done it so enthusiastically. Lauren now had cos-
metic advice from an expert; she had a good speech, a
new nose. It all would work out. Then again, maybe
her speech could be better.

Lauren wet a paper towel with hot water and
applied it to her nose. Then she said to Jennifer,
"Jennifer, could I talk to you a second?"

"Okay, so, like, what have we been doing?"

"You're so popular . . ." Lauren began.

"Yeah," Jennifer agreed.

" 'So, like,' what would you talk about to someone
who's gorgeous?"

"Okay. Like, a guy?"

Lauren spoke carefully. "Possibly."

"Like, I'd like to talk about what I always talk
about—*myself*."

Jennifer turned and walked out. Lauren shook her head in amazement.

Right, she said to herself, *I'll talk to Steve about Jennifer.*

Lauren took the towel off her face. Now her entire nose was bright red.

"Great . . . Rudolph, the red-nosed reindeer!"

10

Lauren stood in the dress department of the most exclusive store in the city.

Elegance! she thought. *I can't stand elegance. I should have brought Patty along to help me withstand the onslaught. But I'm not speaking to Patty Greene! And besides, buying a dress for a romantic confrontation with a janitor wasn't in our popularity plan.*

Lauren fingered a black silk dress.

"Lovely, isn't it?" said a saleswoman, who was suddenly breathing down Lauren's neck.

"Yes, yes, it certainly is," said Lauren.

"Would you care to try it on?" asked the woman.

"Well, I don't know if it's really *me*," said Lauren.

The woman looked at Lauren slowly, taking her in from head to toe. "Perhaps you're right," she said. "You're looking for the real you, I gather?"

"Oh, definitely," said Lauren.

"Is this for a particular occasion?" asked the woman.

"Oh, yes," said Lauren. "The most important occasion of my life so far."

"And you're thinking elegance, aren't you?" said the woman.

"Well, uh."

"What I'm saying," said the woman with a knowing smile, "is you don't want a dress *to sweep floors* in!" The woman laughed.

"I'm not sure about that," said Lauren.

The woman laughed again. "You teen-agers know how to hold up your end of a clever conversation, don't you?" she said. "Well then, let's say you don't want a dress to *wash windows* in!"

"I'm not sure about that either," said Lauren.

The woman stepped backward. "You're sounding serious," she said. "We are on the same wavelength, aren't we? We *are* thinking elegance?"

"How about casual elegance?" said Lauren. "Like, if I got *stranded* somewhere. Say I was taking an elevator to a fancy party on the eighty-fifth floor in an *elegant* skyscraper, but the elevator malfunctioned, and I found myself going down instead of up. I found myself in the *basement*. Then say that someone came to fix the elevator, and there I was standing in it in the dress I'm going to buy here. I would want that person who is going to fix the elevator I'm stuck in to respond to me as a worthy human being, someone deserving of being freed from an elevator prison. So I would want to be wearing something that would bring out a feeling of rapport with the *elevator fixer*. Do you have a rapport dress of that nature?"

"I think you want our sales corner," said the woman. "Discards, seconds, for the woman on her way *down*."

"Now you're talking," said Lauren.

11

The next day Lauren was standing outside the cage in the janitor's area. She was wearing her new outfit. *I'm the first girl in the history of Weemawee High School to buy new clothes to wear to the janitor's area*, she thought. *I could start a trend—Cage Couture.*

Lauren mouthed her speech quickly to make sure she remembered all of it. Then she took a deep breath and raised her arm to knock on the door of the cage.

Ms. Loomis suddenly appeared beside her. "Poor dear," said Ms. Loomis. "This must be a painful time for you. Let's have a little talk, shall we?"

"I have something to do in private, Ms. Loomis."

"In the basement?" said Ms. Loomis. "As someone wiser—so *much* wiser—and older—a tiny bit older—I want to give you some guidance in your little 'affair of the heart.' "

Ms. Loomis grabbed a mop. "Think of this as a symbol," she said. "Mop up your life. Sweep away those bits and pieces of foolishness—"

Lauren tried to grab the mop. "Don't touch this," said Ms. Loomis. "You'll only be hurt, dear."

"By a mop?"

"By the mop's pusher. There is no future! When you're thirty, he'll be forty. When you're forty, he'll be fifty. When you're fifty . . ."

"He'll be *eighty*," said Lauren. "After forty I intend to lie about my age."

What a *good* idea," said Ms. Loomis. She fingered the mop. "I really think that Steve would feel terrible if he knew all the time you were wasting on him."

"Don't mangle that mop," said Lauren. "He's got to do the third floor at two thirty."

"*Two forty-five*," said Ms. Loomis.

"Well, if you stick around here, you'll see how much he likes me," said Lauren.

Ms. Loomis put the mop back. "Sometimes you *have* to be cruel to be kind. Lauren, dear, if you ever want further counsel, I'm always free. In fact, *I* have a marvelous therapist *you* might enjoy. We even see each other socially." Ms. Loomis sighed. "I'll just stay right here to pick up the pieces."

Lauren raised her arm again to knock on the door of the cage. "I'm so nervous."

"Why?" asked Ms. Loomis very sweetly. "Because of that little pimple on your nose?" Ms. Loomis took Lauren's hand. "It's not too late to turn back. No one will think less of you."

Lauren squared her shoulders and knocked on the door.

There was a muffled answer. "Come in."

Lauren walked in. Ms. Loomis followed. They saw a pair of legs. He was standing on a ladder. The rest of him was stuck up into a crawl space in which he was hammering something. Lauren went over and stood close to his feet. *It feels wonderful to be so close to the feet of the man you love,* she thought. *I wonder if I should add that sentiment to my speech. No, a plan is a plan, and my speech is already rehearsed.*

Lauren took another deep breath. "I want to talk to you," she said. "It's Lauren."

"And Allison," Ms. Loomis added.

His muffled voice replied, "Can't come down. . . . Sorry, I've got nails in my mouth."

"Oh. That's okay. Actually that's better. Because, uh, what I have to say is kind of embarrassing, and maybe it's better if I don't say it face-to-face."

"*Uhmmph.*"

"I know it sounds silly, but I truly believe in love at first sight, and from everything I've observed about you these past days I just feel there could be a meaningful relationship between us, and I know I'm kind of young, but I would save myself for you, so . . . I'm yours, if you want me."

Ms. Loomis said, "Wine, like love, is better when it's ripe and mature. Wouldn't you rather have a full-bodied Burgundy than a three-point-two beer?"

She looked pointedly at Lauren.

Lauren had never felt so nervous in her life. She didn't like the way her speech turned out. It had sounded so eloquent directed to the ladies' room mirror. But the die was cast. Why didn't Steve come down? It seemed like an eternity just standing there, waiting.

Finally he bent down. It was *old Mr. Stepanowicz.* It wasn't Steve!

He was looking them over, smiling. "You both look pretty good," he said, "but could you wait till I get my strength back? When you have a heart attack, they like you to kind of put your sex life on hold."

Lauren was mortified. Ms. Loomis was horrified. "Oh, my gosh, where's Steve?" asked Lauren. "I mean, I thought . . . you were—"

Lauren turned and bumped into the door. She had to get out of there. It was too embarrassing. She knocked down all the mops in her haste. She tried to pick them up. But she gave up and ran out.

Mr. Stepanowicz looked confused. This girl had just made him the best offer he had had in about thirty years. It was the only offer he had had. He straightened his bifocals and looked at Ms. Loomis up close. "You can stay, cutie. Actually I prefer beer, but in your case I'll make an exception."

Lauren ran up the stairs and bumped into Patty, who was on her way down.

"Lauren, you look awful. What's wrong?"

"Oh, I just did the dumbest thing, I made this whole speech to Steve's legs, only it was his father's legs, and I made a fool of myself, and I'll never see him again because he's in the woods . . . and . . . hey— what am I doing? I'm not even speaking to *you*!"

Lauren rushed off. She felt more upset than ever.

Patty sank down on the stairs. What in the world had Lauren done? Making a speech to someone's legs didn't seem like the best idea. It was something Jennifer might do. "Like, I like your legs because, you know, like, they're standing on their own two feet."

Patty sighed.

12

When school was over for the day, Lauren walked out of the building dejectedly. Patty was walking alone behind her. Suddenly Lauren's face lit up. There was old Mr. Stepanowicz and Steve unloading some supplies from Steve's pickup truck.

Lauren quickly fixed her hair and turned on one of the smiles she had practiced in front of the mirror. She rushed up to Steve and touched his arm.

He turned.

"Steve! Hi . . . oh, I thought I'd never see you again. I was so miserable, and now you're here and—"

Steve looked at her blankly, puzzled. "Do I know you?"

He didn't know her. He didn't recognize her! She didn't exist. It all came to Lauren in one blast. She pulled back.

"Uh, never mind. Sorry, my *mistake*."

Lauren rushed away.

Steve watched her for a moment, then shrugged, got into his truck, and drove away.

Lauren stood behind a tree and watched him go. Then she looked down at her folder. She slowly raised it to her lips and kissed it good-bye. She dropped it into a garbage can.

Patty rushed up to her. "What happened? You're not talking to me, but I'm talking to you."

Lauren looked at Patty. Then she started to cry. "I'm so miserable!"

Patty and Lauren moved toward each other. They hugged.

They both spoke at once. "I'm sorry. I missed you. It's all my fault."

"You go first," said Patty.

"No, you can," said Lauren.

"Okay," said Patty. "I admit—I left your folder for just one second, and I *tried* to get it back from Jennifer, but by then it was too late. Maybe *unconsciously* I took my eye off it because deep down I didn't think it was a good relationship—not because I'm a snob, but because I thought you'd be hurt—like you are."

"Really? Is that why?"

"I don't know, but it could be."

They both started to laugh. Then Lauren said, "I'm sorry, too. I should have never broken the secret oath, and I should have listened to your explanation. You know, it's no fun having a love affair without you."

"A love affair?"

"A relationship."

"A relationship?"

"Okay, okay," said Lauren. "A fantasy."

"Listen, don't be mad," said Patty. "Can I tell you something? This was one of those 'relationships' that exist *mainly* in your head. There *was* no relationship."

"That's true," said Lauren. She felt depressed. "He didn't even recognize me, Patty. All that, and he didn't even know who I was! I feel so dumb!"

"Don't. Listen. Fantasies are great! 'Fantasy is what makes life livable.' My best friend told me that."

Lauren laughed.

Patty took the discarded folder out of the garbage can and handed it back to her.

"Besides," said Patty, "the best thing about fantasies is you can make them turn out any way you want!"

"I just have this nightmare that I'll really *be* 'sweet sixteen and never been kissed.' Well, I've got two years to go."

13

Patty rushed to answer her telephone. There was always the chance that someone exciting was on the other end. She picked up the receiver.

"Hello."

"Well, hello. Estelle Feiger here."

"You are? I mean, hello. How are you?"

"I think we should drop the formalities and get down to business," said Mrs. Feiger.

"Business?" said Patty.

"Yes, it's about your relationship with Wayne."

"My relationship?" This all was sounding too familiar to Patty. Her relationship with Wayne was about as real as Lauren's had been with Steve Stepanowicz.

"Yes, you had a relationship over a Coke one afternoon, didn't you? Well, since then there's been an abnormally quiet period around here. I asked Wayne when he was going to see you again, but he just flipped his keys and didn't say anything. This is *so* unlike Wayne, who virtually *rushes* home from school each day to tell me everything. So now I'm dependent upon *you*. You'll have to tell me how the relationship has been progressing."

"There's not much to talk about, Mrs. Feiger. As a matter of fact, there's nothing to talk about. Wayne and I had a quotation marks relationship. There are lots of those going around. They're relationships that really aren't."

"Oh, my dear, your pride's been hurt. Estelle Feiger can sense hurt pride right away. I'll try to help. Once again, I reiterate, the color green. I guess you didn't have time to change to green the other day. Also, the expression 'simply stated' is big with Wayne. Prefacing your conversation with 'simply stated' scores points with my Wayne, now, let me see, what can I tell you? Green, 'simply stated,' and perhaps an offhand reference to how shiny he keeps his keys. That's it. Good luck, good health, and don't give up the ship."

Estelle Feiger hung up.

Patty sighed. She deserved to suffer for breaking Rule 3. But when, she wondered, would her suffering ever be over?

14

"How do you think you're adjusting to Weemawee High?" Patty asked Lauren as they were walking down the hall to Ms. Loomis's class.

"I can now look at a waxed floor without thinking of Steve Stepanowicz," said Lauren. "I have this *up* feeling that I'm ready for new challenges."

"Does that mean you could fall for a ceiling painter next?"

"Only if he's Michelangelo." Lauren sighed. "I'm still planning to be popular. But it's hard to meet the right kinds of guys."

"You won't meet them in our next class. Home ec. Oh, I forgot. It's not Home ec anymore. It has a new, improved name." Patty groaned.

"What's wrong with 'Self-sufficiency on Spaceship Earth'?" asked Lauren.

"It barely fits on the blackboard," said Patty. "Plus it's dumb."

"It's supposed to be very *now*."

"Since when is Weemawee now? We're in the eighties, and our school mascot is still an American Indian!"

Lauren and Patty walked into class. The class was composed almost entirely of girls. There were only a couple of boys.

Patty and Lauren took their seats. The classroom subject today was "Self." They knew because Ms. Loomis had written "Self" in enormous block letters on the blackboard.

"Self as in 'my' or 'your'?" Lauren whispered to Patty.

"She'll tell you," said Patty.

"That's what I'm afraid of."

Ms. Loomis started her lecture. A glaze spread over the eyes of most of the students.

Ms. Loomis went on and on, happy to have a tranxfixed, almost hypnotized audience. Finally she summed up. "So you have your choice of three paper assignments for next week. 'When the Relationship Is Over,' 'Between Relationships,' and 'What I Do by Myself When There's No One Else to Do Something with Me.' "

The bell rang.

The students started to get up from their chairs like laboratory animals that had just received a signal to go on to something better.

But Ms. Loomis said, "Friends! Don't leave me yet!"

Everyone looked frustrated. The students sat back down in their chairs.

Ms. Loomis continued. "What I'm about to say is directed only to the women in this room."

Vinnie muttered to Jennifer, "If she starts talking about cramps again, I'm gonna lose my lunch."

Ms. Loomis said, "I've noticed a rather interesting phenomenon over the last few years. All across America women have been moving into areas of endeavor hitherto the sole province of men and their cronies. Medicine, construction work, the Supreme Court—

we've seen the bastions fall, haven't we? Now it's time for us at Weemawee to advance to the final frontier—football.''

The class looked totally confused.

Jennifer looked bored. "Football? You mean, like, with the *ball* and everything?"

"For years, we women have been participating in many sports. But *they* never let us play football. You know why? They don't want us to touch each other. It's a conspiracy. Well, this week at Weemawee we're holding tryouts for an all-women's football team."

LaDonna Fredericks spoke up enthusiastically. "Yeah! And how to return a punt and kick field goals!"

Now Ms. Loomis looked confused. "Are *they* in football?"

Muffy Tepperman stood up. "People, I think it's a wonderful idea. As chairman of the Weemawee Pep Committee, it's my sincere belief that a school with two football teams will be twice as peppy as a school with just one."

Patty whispered to Lauren, "I think that's more pep than the human body can withstand. NASA has exhaustively tested man's pep threshold."

Muffy went on. "Needless to say, I must remove my name from our prospective football roster since my administrative role demands that I take upon myself the duties of coordinating the pep-related activities which, my experience tells me, such a new team as this will require. But irregardless, I will hold myself ready to lend a hand, right from the outset, by proposing a name for our new school team."

Muffy paused dramatically.

"The Weemawee Squaws."

The class moaned and groaned. Some of the students started to hoot.

Muffy looked around. "Well," she said in a huff, "if you think you can improve on that, there'll be a box with a slot in it in the Student Pep Room."

Everyone stood up abruptly and darted out of the room.

15

Jennifer, LaDonna, and Vinnie were at Jennifer's locker. Jennifer was taking books out of her locker and stacking them into Vinnie's arms as if he were a forklift. Everyone talked while Jennifer stacked.

"Come on, girl," LaDonna said to her, "this football team is gonna be a fine time. Get down and hike with the sisters."

Jennifer continued to stack. "I don't know, L.D., you know? Like, I saw this football game on TV once, okay? And this guy was, like, carrying the ball, and everything, you know? And then, like, these two other guys came up behind him and knocked him down into the, like, mud? Like, they completely wrecked his pants."

"Hey, that's part of the game," said LaDonna. "You get new pants later."

"How come you wanna join the team, L.D.?" asked Vinnie.

"I figure it'll be a good career move for me. A lot of people go right from football into show business."

"Oh, yeah?"

"I don't lie. In five years, I could be doing Bob Hope specials and light beer commercials.!"

"Dream on," said Vinnie. "If God had wanted women to play football, he would've made them men instead."

"I don't even *listen* to that jive. Come on, Jennifer. What do you say?"

Jennifer stacked another book. "Okay, like, I don't think it's for me, L.D. It might give me too many muscles, like, where they don't belong. Then what'll I do in the spring—when it's tube top season?"

"That's the right attitude, babe," said Vinnie. "I've got enough muscles for the both of us."

Jennifer tossed one final book on the stack Vinnie was carrying. He buckled under the weight and collapsed to the ground.

16

Patty and Lauren were sitting in the cafeteria, having lunch.

"Why do I have to explain it to you?" Lauren asked. "This football thing is perfect!"

"Perfect? As in what?"

"As in a perfect way to meet the boys' football team! *Duhhn!*"

Patty looked exasperated. "*Lauren . . .*"

"Will you listen to me? We'll be out on that field *every day*—running with them, *breathing* with them, *sweating* with them! It's the ideal atmosphere for romance!"

"Are you in another dimension? Guy jocks don't go for girl jocks. They go for cheerleaders."

"How do you know? Have you ever actually *been* a cheerleader?"

Patty sighed. "All I know is what I read over the sink in the girls' bathroom."

Marshall and Johnny walked over and sat down.

"Hi, beautiful. You, too, gorgeous," said Marshall. "How's my favorite audience today?"

"Chewing our lunch," said Patty.

"Ouch! I love that! Have to use that! Write it down for me, willya, Johnny?"

"Which part? The chewing or the lunch?"

Johnny gazed out into space as he thought about chewing and lunch. It seemed to him a cosmic decision.

"The whole thing, pal," said Marshall. "So what's happening, gals? Why the freezeroo? Was it something I thought?"

"This is a *private* discussion," said Patty.

"Patty won't join the football team with me," said Lauren.

"Wow," said Johnny. "That's a totally different team. Totally. A herd of girls in helmets running into each other and getting hurt? That's so real."

"This is beautiful!" said Marshall. "I can do the

play by play over the PA system! I do a great Howard
Cosell. Listen. 'Well, Muhammad, I understand that
you've moved into a new weight class, and for your
next bout—' "

"You sound like Cary Grant with a different nose,"
said Patty.

"Hey! Great bit!" said Marshall. "I can do Cary
and Cosell together. Perfect combo. Listen. 'Dandy,
dandy, dandy.' "

Marshall turned to Johnny. "I'm gonna be great,
Slash. And you're gonna do the half time show!"

"Oh, *puhleeze* . . ." said Lauren.

Johnny was thinking. "Half time. I like the sound
of that. It sounds so . . . slow."

"Hey, look who's standing on a chair," said Patty,
pointing toward Muffy Tepperman.

"I guess we'll just have to place a marker on that
chair when she's through standing on it," said Marshall. " 'Obnoxious Muffy Tepperman once stood
here.' When you run out of places where George
Washington slept, this could be next in line as a tourist
attraction."

"People!" shouted Muffy. "May I have your attention, please! I have taken it upon myself to find a
consensus as to the name for our new girls' football
team. If you have any suggestions that might be viable,
please submit them to me."

A group of boys shouted, "The Weemawee Wus-
sies!"

Muffy put her hands on her hips. "All right, people, I suppose I'll just have to approach you at another
time when you're not so apathetic."

Lauren muttered, "Muffy doesn't bring out my
apathy. She brings out my hostility. Let's go to math

class and take out our hostility on the substitute teacher. What would we do without subs? We wouldn't have anyone to take advantage of."

17

"I hope this teacher substitute is less pathetic than the one we had in history last week," Patty said to Lauren as they entered math class.

"I wonder what happened to Mrs. Crumholy after she ran out of the school."

"I'm sure she's quit teaching by now and is a quivering mass of jelly." said Patty. "She'll probably wind up a guidance counselor somewhere."

Patty and Lauren took their seats.

A tall, neatly dressed black man was writing on the board. He turned to face the class. They were talking and laughing. They were not paying the slightest attention to him.

Suddenly he whipped a small gun out of his jacket pocket and fired three times over the heads of his class. They were stunned silent. Everyone was terrified.

"That's an old trick I picked up in 'Nam," the substitute teacher said. "Don't worry, they were just blanks. *This* time."

He opened up the gun and discharged the empty shells, which clunked to the ground.

He went on. "The name's Murphy. Osgood Murphy—Platoon sergeant. Oh-six-seven-four-three-eight-nine. Got my discharge in '72, then got into math teaching on the GI Bill. You do your work and leave the area clean, and we'll get along fine. 'Cause nobody wants to be messing with the Big O."

Patty turned to Lauren. "Wonderful. We're being taught algebra by a refugee from *Apocalypse Now*."

"First—story problems. Atten-hut! 'Bomber A can drop its load in two hours; Bomber B, in three hours. How long would it take them if they worked together?' "

The class got busy trying to figure it out. They all were writing furiously. At last Patty raised her hand. She spoke tentatively. "An hour and twelve minutes?"

"An hour and twelve minutes *what*?"

"An hour and twelve minutes of *time*?"

"An hour and twelve mintues, *sir*!"

Patty shrank down in her chair.

"Don't mess with the Big O," said Murphy. "Homework collec-*shun*!"

Murphy started to walk down the first row. Students nervously handed their papers to him. But when he reached Jennifer, she just smiled coyly at him.

"Name!" Murphy barked.

"Jennifer DiNuccio, you know?"

"Where's your assignment, DiNuccio?"

"I couldn't do it. My mother made me organize my lipsticks last night."

"You're not prepared, DiNuccio! Not prepared! And they wonder why Saigon fell! I want you to hand it in tomorrow—ten times!"

Jennifer was taken aback. "For sure," she said.

Murphy moved on to Vinnie, who didn't have a paper either.

"Where's yours, soldier?" Murphy demanded.

"Oh, well, I sort of had football practice last night."

"Football, huh? I played for the Mekong Delta Advisers, back in '62. You a team player, boy?"

"Uh, well, I play on the team, yeah," said Vinnie.

"Then we'll let it slide, Private. At ease."

Murphy moved on.

Everyone, including Vinnie, looked amazed.

After class Patty and Lauren and some of the other girls went to the girls' locker room to change into their football practice gear.

"I wish we had some real uniforms," said Patty. "Our team looks like it was outfitted by the bad will of the Goodwill Industries." There were, of course, the exceptions—Jennifer, who was wearing a designer running suit, and LaDonna, whose football uniform was authentic.

Jennifer spoke up. "I hope they don't expect me to, like, fall down on the grass and that junk. This suit cost a lot of my hard-earned parents' money."

"Haven't you been using it to do aerobics?" asked LaDonna.

"Like, no," said Jennifer. "When I put on an aerobics album, it makes me want to lie down with a diet soda and, like, *listen* to it, you know?"

Muffy walked into the locker room. She went over to Jennifer and LaDonna. "Have you given any thought to a name for our team?" she asked.

"Sure," said Jennifer. "How about the Weemawee Boring Student Leaders, like, would that be good?"

"Jennifer, where were you when school spirit was being given out?"

"Like, was that at the opening of the mall? Like the line, you know, was too long to wait in."

18

Patty and Lauren walked out to the practice fields. "Wait till you see the fields," said Lauren. "The boys' is well groomed, and ours is a dandelion patch. We should call our team the Weemawee Weeds."

The girls' team assembled. Then they trotted out to the field. The boys stopped their playing and gawked.

"Hey! Here comes the pooch Parade!" shouted Vinnie. Then he led the other boys in singing "How Much Is That Doggie in the Window?"

Patty, amazed, turned to Lauren. "So much for the mutual-attraction-of-sweat theory."

"You have no patience!" said Lauren. "These things take time!"

The girls sat down on a bench on their sidelines. Ms. Loomis appeared.

"Well, women," she said, "I hope we have a

productive afternoon. The key to football is being cooperative, supportive, and sensitive to each other's needs—"

There was a loud whistle.

Suddenly Osgood Murphy, in his old army greens, trotted toward them, blowing a gym whistle. He trotted up to Ms. Loomis.

"Osgood Murphy," he announced. "Mathematics. Thought I'd pitch in and give some ground support."

Ms. Loomis gave him a cold look. "Oh, well, that's find, but we *women* were merely trying to discuss the rules in an open, relaxed atmosphere—"

"That won't work," said Murphy bluntly. "Okay, everybody, listen up. Are you combat-ready?"

Ms. Loomis stood there fuming.

Suddenly Muffy ran up to her, carrying a catalog.

"Excuse me, Ms. Loomis—"

"Don't cut in on the Big O," barked Murphy.

But Muffy simply said, "Just a minute, sir," to him and continued to talk to Ms. Loomis. "Ms. Loomis, I think I've found the right uniforms for the team. Aren't these *to die*? Look, they've got the school colors and gold buttons and epaulets—"

Ms. Loomis looked chagrined. "Muffy, I think those are band uniforms."

Muffy drew herself up in a huff. "Well, how was I supposed to know that? No one around here ever gives me constructive input."

"I'm sorry, Muffy," said Ms. Loomis. "I'm sure if we work together, we'll find some *football* uniforms with the school colors."

Murphy spoke up again. "Don't be naïve. School colors are too bright. You need greens, browns, so the enemy won't see you coming out of the tall grass."

Ms. Loomis turned to Murphy. "Mr. Murphy, could we perhaps decide this matter on our own?"

Murphy looked at her intensely. "That's what the Vietcong kept saying."

Ms. Loomis looked flustered. Was she on a football field or a battlefield? Was it perhaps the same? No! This was clearly a place for sensitivity and caring and the exploration of women's potential. She turned to the team. "Everybody, out on the field! Let's play football!"

The girls got up from the bench and trotted out to the field.

19

The girls prepared for a scrimmage. They divided into two huddles.

LaDonna was calling the play inside the first huddle. "Okay, let's try a simple forward pass. Greene, you go out."

"Me?" asked Patty. "Can't I just watch this one?"

"Look, girl," said LaDonna, "I'm the quarterback. You have to do what I say."

Patty whispered to Lauren. "Lauren, *you* go out for the pass. You forced me into this."

"I didn't say I'd catch balls for you!"

"I thought you were my friend!"

"Look," said LaDonna, "I don't have all week. I call 'em like I see 'em."

Patty whispered to Lauren. "If you catch this one, I'll catch the next one."

Lauren rolled her eyes and shrugged.

Now the two teams faced off for the play. LaDonna nimbly faded back for the pass. Lauren started to run down the field. LaDonna threw a beautiful pass.

Lauren caught the ball. She looked amazed at her own feat. She closed her eyes and went running down the field. She used the fact that she was low to the ground to her advantage. She barreled through for a fifteen-yard gain.

One of her opponents clumsily fell down. Lauren tripped over her, ending the play.

Patty ran up to Lauren. "I don't believe you. How did you do that?"

Lauren was elated. "It's easy!" she explained. "Right after you catch the ball, *close your eyes*!"

On the next scrimmage LaDonna faded back, throwing in a few tricky pro football maneuvers this time.

Patty ran downfield. She looked completely terrified.

LaDonna threw the ball in another perfect spiral.

Patty closed her eyes and winced. An instant later the football came toward her. It hit her in the head and sent her glasses flying. She fell to the ground, flat on her back.

Dizzily Patty came to. Everything looked blurry. She tried to focus.

She saw Muffy standing over her. "If you get a

chance between plays," said Muffy, "take the time to think of a name for our team. I'll be in the Pep Shed."

As Patty watched Muffy walk away, she realized there were times when it was better to be unconscious.

Lauren ran over to help Patty to her feet.

"I said to close your eyes *after* you catch it, not *before*," said Lauren.

"I'm quitting! This is *really* dumb!" said Patty. "Where are my glasses? If those lenses popped out again, *so help me . . .*"

"Will you stop it?" said Lauren. "Be positive. Watch this."

Lauren picked up the ball. Then she hurled it in a purposefully clumsy way toward the boys' football field.

A jock noticed it, trotted over to it, and picked it up.

Lauren posed helplessly. Then, with what she hoped was flirtatious sound in her voice, she called out, "Hi! Little help?"

Silently the jock picked up the ball, fired it at Lauren, and trotted away. The ball hit Lauren in the stomach and knocked her over.

"Atrocious aim," she muttered.

On the third scrimmage LaDonna once again expertly faded back for the pass. But this time she couldn't find an open receiver, and she had to look for running room. Out of desperation she lobbed a lateral pass to Jennifer, who was astonished to find a football in her arms.

"L.D.!" she called. "Like, what am I supposed to do with it?"

"Run, girl, run!" shouted LaDonna.

Jennifer started running downfield with the ball.

She was pursued closely by two players. She ran right along the sidelines, adjacent to the boys' field.

She turned and looked in back of her. The two players were gaining on her. *Like, the heat is really on*, she said to herself.

Suddenly she saw Vinnie on the boys' side, in the middle of a play.

"Vinnie!" she shouted.

Jennifer tossed the ball in Vinnie's direction. Vinnie whirled around and, much to his surprise, found a football flying into his arms.

Some of his opponents saw the ball in his arms. They thought it was their game's ball. They were impressed by his agility in capturing the ball so effortlessly, while at the same time they rushed toward him to correct the situation.

They tackled Vinnie and crushed him to the ground in a huge football pileup.

20

"Like, is it never going to be over?" Jennifer asked as the girl's football team dragged themselves through yet another play. They were now thoroughly exhausted, dirty, and roughed up. They were falling over each other.

Only LaDonna was chipper. "Come on, team! Let's do it again!" she yelled.

Ms. Loomis went up to her. "LaDonna, I think we've all worked hard today. Girls, hit the showers."

Murphy came running up. "No way," he said. "This squad hasn't begun to work. I want to see twenty laps, on the double, let's go!"

All the girls groaned and moaned. But they didn't move.

Instantly Murphy whipped out his gun. Three shots rang out. The girls sprang to their feet and started running.

"Let's hear some singing," said Murphy as he began a chant. "We don't want to wear a skirt. We like knee pads, sweat, and dirt."

The girls started chanting.

"Louder," he shouted. "I can't hear you."

Later in the locker room the girls were sitting around, totally worn out. Patty and Lauren were exhausted.

"Next time you want us to meet boys, let's just go to a bar," Patty said to Lauren.

"We can't do that until we're twenty-one."

Patty collapsed on the bench. "Well, I don't plan to stand up until then."

Just then Muffy dashed in. "People," she said, "I've got some wonderful news! Our opponents Friday will be the Mid-Central Colossus." A look of terror spread over the team.

Lauren turned to Patty. "Mid-Central?"

"The toughest school in the tristate area," said Patty.

"Not a good idea. The Big O will shoot us," Lauren said.

"Do we have spirit? Do we have pep?" Muffy called.

"Muffy, the great untouched!" shouted Lauren. "Only her mouth has seen action."

21

Lauren watched while the two school buses, painted a cool blue, drove up the driveway near the football field. On the sides of the buses were painted the words "Mid-Central High School." The bus doors swung open, and lines of tall, athletic-looking girls streamed out.

Lauren stared at them. *I never thought vigor would make me sick*, she thought. *There they are, a tribute to vitamins, glorious genes, and regimen. And foresight*, she added as she saw pro football equipment, headsets, stretchers, and X-ray machines being unloaded. *The stretchers and X-ray equipment are probably for our team. I was taught that giving a gift to a hostess was good manners, but now I wonder. For the girls who have everything—contusions, sprains, broken bones, and torn cartilage . . .*

Lauren watched while the team quarterback ran out of a bus. She was big and blond. Her arm was already cocked for a pass. The rest of the team got off the bus. The black girls went through an extremely complicated sequence of maneuvers. Then the quarterback threw the ball, right on target. The receiver caught the ball and spiked it into the ground.

"Say it isn't so." Lauren groaned. "We're finished before we start."

Lauren rushed back to the Weemawee girls' locker room, where her teammates were changing into their new uniforms. Lauren stared at the uniforms in amazement. "They're our school colors all right, but why have the pants been done in a preppy plaid pattern? And those tops! Our names embroidered in script instead of printed in block letters! We look like a ladies' embroidery class that somehow got entangled with a boys' prep school and everybody lost. Who am I that I should appear on a football field in an embroidered top and plaid bottom? Charlie the Tuna has better taste."

Jennifer spoke up. She looked dissatisfied, too. "L.D., I'm trying to remember something. In football, when do you get new pants?"

"Huh?" said LaDonna. "Oh, that's only if something really bad happens to the pants you have on."

"Well, like, I hope something does. If I found these pants in my closet, I'd call the Gross Patrol."

Suddenly a male voice shouted, "Yo! Is everybody decent in there?"

Some of the girls scrambled for cover. Some wrapped their fully clothed bodies with towels. Jennifer stood up on a bench and said, "Eeek! Like, I would do this for a mouse."

There were screams of "It's a man! Call the police! Gross!"

Suddenly Vinnie appeared in the locker room.

"Oh, it's just Vinnie," said Jennifer coolly.

Everyone relaxed.

"What are you doing in here, Vinnie?" asked LaDonna. "Didn't you see the sign out there that says 'Girls'?"

" 'Women,' " said Lauren. "Ms. Loomis changed it last night."

Vinnie started to jeer. "All right, this whole thing's a joke, right? You're not really gonna play those people out there, are you? They'll stomp on you!"

LaDonna went up to Vinnie. "Hey, Vinnie, disappear."

"Okay, okay. So you're gonna go through with it. Well, then you might as well learn to play like real men. Start snapping some towels around here."

Vinnie picked up a towel. He snapped it against a locker. The towel snapped back at him. "Must be a defective towel," he said.

He picked up another towel. "If you wanna get psyched, start swatting your teammates."

Jennifer collared Vinnie and kicked him out of the locker room.

"Good play," said LaDonna.

22

The team walked out to the bench on the Weema-wee sidelines and sat down.

Ms. Loomis started her lecture. "Women, in a few moments the game will begin. I'm glad we've found this moment alone together because there's one last thing I wanted to tell you. In football, as in life—"

Osgood Murphy suddenly appeared. He was carrying an easel with a diagram on it.

He spoke to the team. "Okay, enough chitchat. It's two minutes till the battle, and I've got one last play to teach you. Now listen up."

Ms. Loomis stepped aside. She was fuming. What did this man know about how closely the game of football and the game of life were related? And now the women of the team would never find out. They would go through life cheated of the connection.

Murphy displayed his football play diagram. "This is the standard X's and O's, but against the backdrop of a map of Vietnam, with the line of scrimmage represented by the demilitarized zone."

Murphy waited for it to sink in. Then he went on. "Okay, the ball's here on the thirty-yard line—due south of Haiphong Harbor. Now, the quarterback—" He turned. "Hey! Where's the quarterback?"

Jennifer pointed to LaDonna, who was off at a distance. "Like, L.D. didn't want to be disturbed. She's kind of psyching herself up." Murphy nodded. "I did that before the Tet offensive."

Out of hearing distance of her team, LaDonna was intense in her concentration. "Hello . . . this is La-Donna Fredericks . . . I want to talk to you about light beer. . . ."

LaDonna lowered her voice, raised her voice, and then tried a medium pitch. What was better—a soft sell, a hard sell, vivacity, aloofness? It was difficult selling light beer across the vastness of America. But after all, that's what they would be paying her an annual six-figure salary for.

Suddenly a voice came over the PA system. Muffy Tepperman was speaking. "People, can I have your attention, please? Can you hear me? This is Muffy Tepperman, chairman of the Weemawee Pep Commit-tee. Over the past week I have been conducting a tireless, thoroughgoing search for prospective names for our new Weemawee team. To my deep chagrin, the number of students offering feasible suggestions has been a good deal lower than I, in my planning stages, had realistically projected. Therefore, an *ad hoc* stu-dent committee of experts in matters of pep had to be assembled to name the team. After hours of serious deliberation this blue-ribbon panel has decided to name the team"—Muffy paused dramatically—"the Weemawee Squaws!"

A round of loud boos rose up from the Weemawee bleachers.

Muffy Tepperman was puzzled. Were those *boos* she was hearing? No! The PA system must be faulty. Poor technology was ruining her moment of glory.

Marshall took over the microphone. Muffy glared at him. It certainly wasn't right just to take away, to *dissipate*, a person's moment of glory. Still, what was one more triumph to her, one more notch on her belt?

She thought of all the committees she had chaired. When she was just four years old, she had been named chairchild of a Stuffed Toys Committee. That had been the beginning of an illustrious chairing career. After that the committees had come along like an inevitable and irresistible force of nature. She had been *meant* to chair. She had been meant to lead! Let Marshall have his little moment of glory with his terrible little jokes. Poor Marshall. Muffy Tepperman was such a hard act to follow!

Marshall spoke into the microphone. "Good afternoon, sports fans. Marshall Blechtman here. It's great to be playing Weemawee High. And how about this new football team, huh? The last time I threw a girl a forward pass, she socked me in the mouth! But seriously—"

Another voice broke in. "Time to begin the game." The game began.

"I don't know what I'm doing," said Patty after the game had been in progress for some time.

"Well, then our team is completely unified," said Lauren. "None of us knows what we're doing, except LaDonna, and I'm not so sure about her anymore."

The Weemawee team was in a huddle.

In a lightning-fast voice LaDonna said, "Okay. Fourteen, drop back on the mean side, slippin', slopin', cantaloupin'. On six."

She broke up the huddle. The other girls looked totally perplexed.

"What did she say?" asked Patty. "What did she *mean*?"

Lauren tried to quiet her down. "Don't act so dumb! We'll figure it out later."

The two teams formed at the line of scrimmage.

The play began. No one on the Weemawee team knew where she was going. LaDonna's instructions buzzed in their heads. "Fourteen, drop back on the mean side, slippin', slopin', cantaloupin'. On six."

"The last time I heard anything like that was in The Grease," muttered Lauren. "And it was on special for breakfast."

LaDonna had to scramble in the backfield. She got tackled by four hulks. She sprang to her feet and got tackled again. She rose once more. "The things you have to do, the compromises you have to make on the road to show biz success," she said, sighing as she examined herself for bruises. "The camera picks up everything. Will the public buy LaDonna Fredericks with welts?"

In the next huddle LaDonna said, "This time get it right." Her lightning-fast voice took over: "Thirty-two split back on the double back side, huffin', puffin', rebuffin' on two."

Once again the Weemawee girls were thoroughly confused.

Out on the field Patty said to Lauren, "I'm going to huff and puff right out of this game."

"I *think* I know what LaDonna means. Wasn't that a line from '*The Three Little Pigs*'?"

"I think so. I haven't read it lately."

"Can you remember the plot?" asked Lauren. "If we knew the plot, we could figure out what LaDonna wants us to do."

"Right now I think we'd better just run," said Patty. "LaDonna is glaring at us."

The Weemawee team continued its newly established tradition of playing in total confusion.

It was time for another scrimmage. LaDonna faded

back, found an opening, and threw the football. The ball bounced off Patty's head and sent her glasses flying out of her helmet.

The ball landed in Jennifer's arm. She was astonished. She was also horrified to see several Mid-Central players running right at her.

Jennifer looked at the ball in terror. "I don't even *want* this gross ball!"

Jennifer threw the ball away. It landed in Lauren's arms. The Mid-Central players started to run after Lauren, Jennifer sighed in relief. "Like, my mascara can run faster than I can."

Lauren was panic-stricken. She closed her eyes and started running like a maniac. She had gained an amazing twenty yards before she was tackled by several large opponents. She moaned and got unsteadily to her feet.

LaDonna felt psyched. "All right!" she said.

Marshall's voice came through the PA system. "You know why all those girls are fighting with each other out there, folks? It's because they all showed up in the same outfit!" He chuckled. Then he said, "Just in case you hadn't noticed, the scoreboard reads 'Weemawee, seven, Visitors, forty-two. And the last few seconds of the first half are ticking away."

Marshall continued while the Mid-Central girls briskly trotted off the field and the Weemawee girls dragged themselves slowly toward their sidelines. "Well, better luck next half, chicks! I have an announcement, will the owner of a Buick Skyhawk, license plate four-three-three-ZPI, please move your car. You're on my foot! Ha! Ha! Just kidding! And now, ladies and gentlemen, sit back and enjoy our half time show—as the Johnny Slash A & M Marching Band performs 'A Musical Salute to Things.' "

Johnny Slash walked leisurely out onto the field. He looked at the crowd, took off his glasses, and put them back on. He was terrified, but he had the half time show to do.

23

Inside the Weemawee locker room everyone looked miserable. Jennifer was trying to make the best of the situation. She was fiddling with her eye makeup.

"Hey, Jennifer," LaDonna called, "you're supposed to put that black grease *under* your eyes."

"Grease?" Jennifer was shocked. "I thought this was shadow! Oh, *make me lose it all!*"

Patty and Lauren were commiserating. "I'm not going out there again!" Patty said.

Lauren felt like gritting her braces. "How can you quit now? That's really dumb."

"I don't intend to quit," said Patty. "I'm going to get *excused*."

Patty walked up to Ms. Loomis.

"Uh, Ms. Loomis . . . could I talk to you a minute?"

"Yes, Patty? What is it?"

Patty had trouble finding the words. She didn't find

the words. Finally, she said, "My . . . um . . . 'visitor' is here."

"What visitor is that?" asked Ms. Loomis.

"No, no . . . you see, I think it's my *time*. My 'little friend.' The *curse*."

"Time? Curse?" said Ms. Loomis. "What are you talking about?"

"Ms. Loomis, it's that *time of the month*."

The shock of recognition passed across Ms. Loomis's face. "Oh! I see! I see!" Ms. Loomis pulled Patty aside. She spoke softly but intensely. "Don't let any men hear you say that! They'll never let you be President!"

"But—"

"It's true that we women need a little more iron every month," said Ms. Loomis. "But that shouldn't get in the way of what's important to us—like football."

Ms. Loomis took out a bottle that was in her shirt pocket. She unscrewed the cover and poured a handful of pills into Patty's hand. "These have all the minerals you need."

Patty looked frustrated. "I don't want minerals. I want to be excused. *Excused*. I promise I'll eat raisins every month if you excuse me this time."

Ms. Loomis didn't hear her. She had moved on to address the team.

"Women! Women! Could I talk to you for a moment? The first half is over, and we've scored one touchdown. That's a wonderful achievement—"

Out of nowhere Osgood Murphy suddenly appeared. Some girls tried to cover themselves up, but they stopped. They were too tired to do anything.

Murphy's voice filled the room. "Let's cut it, you

girls were playing like girls out there. I want to see you shape up—and I mean now."

Ms. Loomis was furious. "Mr. Murphy, I've had about enough of this! Who give you the right to interfere with this team?"

Ms. Loomis was proud of her assertiveness. She had been searching for a suitable female role model. She had gone through Eleanor Roosevelt, Indira Gandhi, Golda Meir, Joan Crawford, Wonder Woman, and Jane Austen. She had finally settled on—herself. If not me, who? *Whom*?" she asked herself. This Mr. Murphy now had to realize he was dealing with a formidable opponent!

Murphy stared her down. "Don't mess with the Big O," he boomed. Then he turned to the girls. "Now back to the field!"

The girls wearily picked themselves up and dragged themselves out to the playing field. Johnny Slash was on the field, performing his half time show.

Marshall was announcing, "For his next number Johnny will contort his body into the shapes of the states of Texas, Arkansas, and Rhode Island."

Johnny seemed unfazed by the challenge. Possibly he didn't know what state he was in anyway. He moved, twisted, and rolled his body into several strange, totally unrecognizable shapes.

Marshall continued. "For his next number Johnny will contort his body into the shape of your favorite city and mine. Johnny, show us what that city is!"

Johnny once again moved, twisted, and rolled his body into several strange, totally unrecognizable shapes.

Marshall's voice was awash in admiration. "Wasn't that great, folks? What a humanitarian! And now for his final number Johnny Slash in a tribute to Weemawee High School, will spell 'Weemawee High School.' "

Johnny started to spell out the words by forming his body into the shapes of the different letters: *W, E, M, A, W*—

Marshall's voice broke through nervously. "Uh, Johnny . . . I think you left out the second *E*."

Johnny wobbled his head vaguely, lamenting his lost *E*. He had lost it *totally*. Johnny hurriedly ran back, "erased" his letters, and started all over again.

A loud buzzer sounded. It was the signal for the start of the second half of the game. The two teams moved onto the field. Johnny continued to spell. "I'm not finished! I'm not finished!" he yelled as two big, strong players from Mid-Central ran to Johnny, lifted him up, and carried him off the field.

Marshall's voice came through the PA system. "What a finale! What a man! Johnny Slash! I love that guy!"

The two teams lined up for the kick-off. Mid-Central kicked a booming kick, and the Mid-Central team advanced downhill for the kill, knocking over everybody they saw.

The ball hit Jennifer in the foot, and she tripped and fell into a patch of mud. "Jennifer DiNuccio in Gross City!" she said in disgust.

The ball continued to roll into the end zone as, one by one, the entire Weemawee team was flattened.

Jennifer picked herself up and started running off the field. "Like, I could have been at the mall," she complained. She headed for the showers.

A few other Weemawee girls furtively started to run off the field. LaDonna looked perplexed. "Hey! Where's everybody going?"

Patty and Lauren looked at each other. Then they started to head off the field.

Patty said, "Be honest. Was joining this team really worth it?"

"Well," said Lauren, "how many days of the week do we get to see Jennifer fall facedown into mud?"

"All right," said Patty. "It was worth it."

They headed for the showers. "We'll have to talk about our future at Wemawee High," said Lauren. "When I was out there on the field, I relived all the bad moments of my life. Like when I had my consultation with the orthodontist and he looked at me solemnly and said, 'Braces!' "

"What does that have to do with our future at Weemawee?" asked Patty.

"Well, when I think of something depressing, I immediately try to think of something that's the opposite. Braces are depressing, and popularity is the exact opposite of braces."

"It *is*?"

"It is when you wear braces. So anyway, out there on the football field I thought about how very popular you and I are going to be at Weemawee. This school is going to *appreciate* Patty Greene and Lauren Hutchinson!"

"It *is*? *How*?"

"Haven't the vaguest idea," said Lauren as they walked into the showers.

24

The Weemawee team was in mass flight from the football field.

Marshall spoke into the microphone from the PA booth. His voice had what he hoped was the unmistakable sound of Howard Cossell. "Ladies and gentlemen, in all my years in sports I have never seen anything remotely like what I have seen here today. Mid-Central wins by forfeit. Back to you—"

Muffy grabbed the microphone away from him. "Your attention! Your attention!"

The Weemawee girls continued to pour off the field.

Muffy's voice shrieked. "Get back on the field! Start playing! This is an outrage! This is student apathy at its worst! This is . . . treason against pep!"

As if prompted, the girls picked up their pace. They ran off the field as fast as they could.

LaDonna was left alone on the field. Two girls from Mid-Central ran up to her. The first girl said, "Hey! Don't feel bad!"

"Why shouldn't I?" said LaDonna glumly. "I lost the game . . . and I lost my team. Now I'll probably never get to do commercials."

"Look, you can join our team anytime you want," said the second girl.

LaDonna looked at the girl skeptically. "Oh, right. You're just saying that 'cause I'm a sister."

"No way!" said the second girl. "We saw you play! You were slick!"

"Really?" said LaDonna.

"Yea," said the first girl. "If you want to transfer to Mid-Central, you could be our quarterback!"

LaDonna was amazed. "Wow . . . that's real nice . . . but I guess I kind of belong here. If I were at Mid-Central, I'd be a little fish in a big pond. Here at Weemawee I'm the coolest girl in the school."

"*That's* the truth," said the second girl.

"Anyway, you guys don't need a quarterback!" said LaDonna. "The one you've got throws like an ace!"

"Yeah," said the first girl. "She's pretty good at throwing . . . but she's got problems."

"Like what?" asked LaDonna.

"Well, for one thing," said the first girl, "when she's in the huddle, we can never understand anything she's saying."

LaDonna and the two girls walked off the field together.

25

Patty dragged herself wearily across the room to answer the phone. Who could it be? Probably a dry-cleaning establishment soliciting business from the Weemawee girls' football team.

Maybe it was someone soliciting for a major medical plan, inspired, no doubt, by the performance of the girls' football team. Then again it could be Osgood Murphy, calling to tell her that although the battle was lost, the war still remained to be fought.

"Hello."

"Estelle Feiger here."

"No!"

"What?"

"I said, 'Oh.' "

"Yes, well, I called to say I watched each and every move you made during the football game with Mid-Central High. I was sitting in the bleachers. I went alone. Wayne doesn't like football. So I went for him."

"You didn't have to do that."

"Wait until you're a mother. You do these things. School spirit. Somebody has to have it."

"I guess."

"I called for a couple of reasons. First, to say that I admired your performance on the football field."

"Thank you."

"And the second reason . . ." Mrs. Feiger's voice trailed off.

"Your second reason?" Patty prompted her. She really didn't want to hear it. But she knew it would be coming. Tidal waves are not to be denied.

"This is delicate, my dear Patty," said Mrs. Feiger.

"That's okay."

"Well, no, it isn't. You see *I* think that you're right for my Wayne. I can see you going through the years together, married, having children, sharing your life's accomplishments and problems. That's what *I* can see. Please believe me."

"I do."

"But I have this nagging sense that it just wasn't meant to be. There's been no movement since that date over a Coke. Time has passed."

"Oh, so that's the second thing you wanted to tell me. That Wayne and I probably don't have a future together. Well, Mrs. Feiger, I think you're right. I know you're right. And it's been wonderful having these various telephone conversations with you from time to time. I wish you and Wayne good luck in all your future endeavors."

"Wait!" said Mrs. Feiger. "You've got the second reason all wrong."

"Don't say that," Patty wailed.

"Well, I do agree that you and Wayne probably don't have a future together. But I called for another reason. I saw another girl at the football game who I think, in all honesty, Wayne should lose no time in asking for a date."

Patty was groaning to herself. *Oh, don't let it be Lauren. What if Mrs. Feiger was impressed by her twenty yards.*

"The girl I have in mind speaks with exceptional clarity. She seems to have goals and a sense of herself. Who she is, where she's going."

Patty wondered. Could she mean LaDonna Fredericks? LaDonna was the most outstanding person on the team. She was the only outstanding person on the team.

Then again maybe it was Jennifer. She certainly has a sense of herself, and only herself, although it would be hard to describe her as speaking with exceptional clarity.

"Do you have the telephone numbers of the girls?" asked Mrs. Feiger. "I'm calling to get the number of that girl for Wayne. Actually I need her name, too."

Patty felt new hope go through her. Mrs. Feiger would have another number to call. Patty would be dropped from her list. She might never hear from Mrs. Feiger again!

"I'll give you any number I can, Mrs. Feiger. Any number."

"Oh," said Mrs. Feiger, "Wayne is losing a treasure in you."

"Those are the breaks," said Patty.

"Well, I guess I don't have to tell you what girl is your replacement."

"I guess not," said Patty. "She's the one with the mascara, right?"

"I didn't notice what she wears on her eyes, and I didn't catch her name, but she's Chairman of the Weemawee Pep Committee," said Mrs. Feiger.

"Ooooooh," said Patty. *"That* one. You're right,

Mrs. Feiger. She and Wayne, well, they could certainly go down the road of life together. The *name's* Muffy Tepperman. The number's in the book. Good luck, good health, and don't give up the ship."

Patty hung up. *I just now completely recovered from that football game* she decided.

26

Patty and Lauren were standing in line in the cafeteria.

"Are we popular?" Patty asked Lauren. "We've been at Wemawee High for weeks, and I still don't know."

"I think when you're popular, you know it." said Lauren. "Popularity sort of grabs you like static cling. You feel it when you've got it."

"I'm not sure I'm anywhere," said Patty. "Sometimes I think about Vinnie, but when I do, I think about Jennifer."

"Erase that last thought, said Lauren. "Like, you know, eradicate it, like." Lauren laughed. "I'm totally over Steve Stepanowicz, and I'm over that football game. Those were my two lows of the year so far."

"Speaking of lows . . ." said Patty, looking around.

"I see them," said Lauren. "Here come the two all-time lows of all time, Marshall Blechtman and Johnny Slash. Let's eat and run."

Lauren quickly filled up her food tray. Patty looked down and made a face. "I don't know how you can eat the Weemawee pasta of the day. It looks like what my mother used to caulk the bathroom tiles."

"Patty, pasta is one of the most nutritionally sound foods you can eat. Besides, I'm taking starch blockers."

"The Green Bay Packers couldn't block that starch," said Marshall, looking over Lauren's shoulder.

"Hello and good-bye, Marshall," said Lauren.

She and Patty took their food trays and started to walk toward a table. "Hey, wait, Patty," said Lauren. "Look at that poster."

Patty looked up at a handmade poster. "MUFFY TEPPERMAN, ASSISTANT DIRECTOR, ANNOUNCES AUDITIONS FOR THE WEEMAWEE AUTUMN MUSICAL, WRITTEN AND DIRECTED BY DRAMA TEACHER EXTRAORDINAIRE MR. JON-MICHAEL SPACEK. CREATIVITY + SCHOOL SPIRIT = A BIG HIT."

Patty looked at Lauren suspiciously. "Please forget it."

"Forget what? I didn't say anything."

Patty started to walk away from the poster. "Good," she said.

"I was just thinking how lucky you are to be so musical," said Lauren. "I can't even carry a tune. Patty, your voice is a real gift—"

"Some gift. I'd rather have my own phone."

Patty and Lauren sat down at a table. "You shouldn't take your talent for granted," said Lauren as she took a large forkful of pasta.

"I don't," said Patty, "but what good does it do me?"

"Don't you see? You could be a star, and there's nothing that assures popularity like stardom. Look at Ronald Reagan."

"Are you saying that if I star in the Weemawee Autumn Musical, in seventy-five years I could be president?" asked Patty dubiously.

"You never know," said Lauren.

Patty looked up. Marshall and Johnny were standing there, listening.

"C'mon, Patty, try out," said Marshall as he and Johnny sat down. "I'm going to. There's nothing like a live audience. Even Johnny Slash is going to try out."

"Hi, guys!" said Muffy, holding a stack of index cards.

She looked at Patty. "Hi, string bean."

She looked at Lauren. "Hi, fang."

Johnny instinctively put on his sunglasses and turned up his Walkman. He was now effectively shielded against Muffy Tepperman.

"Muffy," said Marshall, "when you're seventy-five, are people still going to call you Muffy, as in Grandma Muffy, Grandpa Skip?"

"Wow," said Johnny, "I never thought of that . . . Grandpa Johnny . . . Gramps Slash . . . Pop-Pop Johnny. . . ."

"I'm going to ignore that," said Muffy, "because, as you see, I am carrying *index cards*! What do these index cards, green, pink, and blue, mean to Weemawee High School? A very great deal, people! As you know, I am the assistant director of the Weemawee Autumn Musical, which was written especially for us by Mr. Jon-Michael Spacek. Of course, we all want to participate, don't we? Now stagehands get green cards, ticket sellers get blue cards, and acting hopefuls get pink cards. For example, in awareness of talent, I have just given Jennifer a pink card for actress. Now, Patty, I'm pleased to be giving you a blue card for the ticket-selling committee."

"Muffy," said Lauren, "Patty wants a pink card. She's going to audition."

"I think she should," said Muffy. "If she can deal with rejection, that is. Sorry if the truth hurts."

"Muffy," said Lauren, "I've been meaning to ask you, is that your real nose?"

Muffy glared at Lauren. She handed Patty a pink card. "I think she should try out even if the outcome is inevitable." Then she turned and marched away.

"I wasn't too rude to Muffy, was I?" asked Lauren.

"It's impossible to be *too* rude to Muffy," said Patty.

"That's the spirit, kiddo," said Marshall. "When you're on your way to stardom, you've got to be rude, selfish, inconsiderate, ungrateful, spiteful, malicious—"

"No, there's no excuse for bad manners," Johnny said, picking up Marshall and carrying him off.

"Listen," said Lauren. "The best thing about stepping on the people you meet on the way up is that you get to step on them again on the way down."

"That's two times too many," said Patty.

Lauren sighed. "You just don't understand the responsibilities of stardom."

27

Jon-Michael Spacek, the drama teacher of Weemawee High, was dressed in his usual calculatedly casual manner. It was rumored that he spent two hours every morning trying to look as if he had spent ten minutes getting dressed. A thin tie hung loosely around his neck. The sleeves of his designer shirt were neatly rolled up.

Mr. Spacek was passing out scripts to the students who were clustered in twos and threes around the auditorium.

Muffy was trying to get everyone's attention. "All right, people . . . I'm in charge. I know we're . . . all atwitter but let's try to contain ourselves . . . Good news, people. Mr. Spacek, our fantastically talented director, has generously promised to donate half the ticket money to our adopted Guatemalan child. After all, our child has taken Weemawee as her communion name, and sending her that other shoe is the least we can do in return. And now . . . I'd like to introduce to you . . . Jon-Michael Spacek, our director."

"Fellow thespians—" said Mr. Spacek.

"Hey, who you calling a thespian?" yelled Vinnie.

"Theater is hard, thankless work," said Mr. Spacek. "How many of you have seen *All That Jazz*? Good. Then you know what I mean. To you this is just another school event, but to me this is the Great White Weemawee Way."

"White?" said LaDonna.

Vinnie called from the audience. "Yo, Space Case."

Jennifer was confiding to LaDonna. "Okay, don't you, like, think that, like, Mr. Spacek is, you know, like, kind of, like *you know* . . you know?"

"What're you talking about, girl?" said LaDonna. "The man's got six kids."

"Yeah, like okay, but he's still sort of, you know, a—you know."

"What do I hear out there, people?" called Muffy. "Do I hear whispers and giggles? Do I hear the sounds of *childhood*? Mr. Spacek is addressing you, the artistic cream of Weemawee. He is under the impression that you have reached *peoplehood*. Let us show him that he is right. A generous round of silence will be appreciated, punctuated by applause at the appropriate places. Once again, Mr. Spacek."

"Thank you, Muffy. I want to convey to all of you what Muffy instinctively understands. My standards are high."

Vinne called from the audience. "I thought just your voice was high."

Mr. Spacek went on. "Do you know, when I first set foot on Broadway, the truly great actors were still around? Carol Channing. Theodore Bikel. Don't get me started. It was exciting at first. Opening nights at Sardi's, late suppers at the Algonquin. We thought we were the new wits of the Round Table. And we were. But the dream soured and died, as most dreams do. Good theater was no longer important. Good reviews were all that mattered. How could I live in a city like that? How could I survive? And that, my new best friends, is how I came to Weemawee. So you see, leaving Broadway was not an end; it was a beginning."

Mr. Spacek made a circle sign with his hands. Then he continued. "High school is painful on both sides of the desk. I was here, and I know. But now I have captured this torment in a bold new musical. *A Cafeteria Line*. I'm going to do to high school what *A Chrous Line* did to Broadway."

Patty started to get up. Lauren pushed her back down.

"Like all great stories, it is a love story," said Mr. Spacek. "It comes from here." He touched his head. "And here." He touched his heart. "And here." He touched his stomach.

Vinnie yelled, "Stop right where you are."

Mr. Spacek clapped his hands. "Now, darlings, it's—he waved his hands around—"audition time! There will be no pushing or screaming. You will, each and every one of you, have a chance to show us what you can do up there on the stage. First the three girls in the tutus and then the mime with the invisible dog. After that Marshall Blechtman."

"I'm following an invisible dog?" said Marshall.

Mr. Spacek sat back. Muffy was sitting beside him, carrying a clipboard.

When Marshall's turn came, he ran up onto the stage, and when he turned to face the audience, he was wearing a bad wig. He was certain he was using his best Roseanne Roseannadanna voice. "Last night I had a little teensy-weensy, itsy-bitsy piece of spinach, it was disgusting, Jane—I thought I was going to die."

"No, no, no!" cried Mr. Spacek. "Geniuses are a glut in the theater. Everywhere you look, another one. I'm not seeing what I want to see. I want to see pain. Give me pain. Real pain."

"Pain?" said Marshall. "I'll tell you pain. There's no one good to imitate anymore. No Cagneys, no Bogarts, no . . ." Marshall imitated Cary Grant. "Judy, Judy, Judy."

"Next!" screamed Mr. Spacek.

Marshall walked back to his seat. "The best stand-up comic in Weemawee High School is being ordered to sit down! It will all go into my autobiography tentatively titled *They All Laughed at Marshall Blechtman Except Jon-Michael Spacek.*"

LaDonna Fredericks was on the stage. "I am prepared, Mr. Spacek. I have written an original poem. It is called 'There Ain't a Black Girl Alive Who Can Look at a Broom and Think About Halloween.' I will begin. 'My mama, my mama, my mama rode the bus. . .'"

Mr. Spacek was full of soul. "Talk to me, sister. Get down with your bad self."

LaDonna looked stunned.

Mr. Spacek screamed, "Next!"

LaDonna walked off the stage just as Jennifer was walking on. LaDonna grabbed Jennifer. "Listen," she said, "theater spoils you for TV commercials anyway. Makes you too classy. And theater pays peanuts compared to telling the great unwashed what deodorant to use. You got trouble under your armpits? You can get a few hundred thousand if you're the armpits' spokesman. Shampoo's good, too. Conditioners pay even better. It's the best of all possible times to do commercials."

"Girls are always asking me what products *I* use," said Jennifer. "But I believe in being natural, you know, like, I eat Grape-nuts."

Jennifer stood on the stage. "Like, all I want to say

is that, like, if I'm not, like, the star, like, I'd rather just, like, go to the mall, okay?''

"Jennifer," said Mr. Spacek, "I want you to share a trauma with me. Trauma? You know, bad thing?''

"Yeah, well, like, when I was, you know, in seventh grade, like, I was the only girl, like, who had a, you know, date for the, like, sock hop.''

"And that was traumatic?" Mr. Spacek looked perplexed.

"Well, like, it was for all the other girls, you know?''

"No, no, no!" said Mr. Spacek. "Surely something bad has happened to you . . . once?''

"Okay, fine, but like, I don't like talking about it, okay? Once I, like, left my makeup, you know, in the car at the beach, okay? And like, you know, it was real hot, and like, it melted and everything. I mean, like, I *cried*.''

Mr. Spacek screamed, "Next!" Then he covered his head with both hands and softly moaned. "Another entry in Jon-Michael's amateur hour. I don't know why I ever thought I wanted to get into theater. Everyone *loves* my clothes. I could have been a famous designer. My name would have been on everyone's lips and possibly on everyone's back pocket.''

Vinnie strutted up to the stage. "Okay, I wanna sing a song that really comes from here.'' He touched his heart. "This song is so important they sing it before every Yankees game.''

"The national anthem," said Mr. Spacek. "Interesting choice.''

"Nah," Vinnie said. He opened his mouth and sang a fabulous rendition of "New York, New York.''

Patty, back in the audience, said to Lauren, "I

can't stand it. He can sing, too. He's too much."

"Patty," said Lauren, "it's okay to have a Little Crush on Vinnie. But please, no more Big Crushes. Remember Larry Simpson, the senior you salivated over? If you want to be popular, you have to be cool. *You* be the star. Let everybody else be star-struck."

"Over *me*?"

"Sure. You just have to believe in yourself."

Johnny Slash leaned over Patty's shoulder. "That's good advice," he said. "I believe in myself. Whoever I may be."

"Well, when you find out who that is, let us know," said Lauren.

"Johnny Slash, the Great Unknown!" said Marshall. "A hand, ladies and gentlemen, for this man who has come so far with so little!"

"Darlings, out there! Quiet, please!" Mr. Spacek was waving his arms as if any army of fleas had suddenly descended on him. "A little respect and appreciation for Mr. Pasetta!"

When Vinnie was finished, he strutted off the stage and up the aisle. Mr. Spacek rushed up the aisle after him, screaming, "I am dying!" He ran up to Vinnie. "Do you know what I'm thinking right now? You are the only logical choice to play the Drama Teacher."

Vinnie looked puzzled. "The lead?"

"Yes. You're a rich, untapped reservoir of talent."

Jennifer whispered to LaDonna, "Like, he likes that lower hanging lip of Vinnie's. Do you know how many famous actors have lower hanging lips? Like, it's, you know, eleven out of ten. I counted."

Mr. Spacek said, "The quality of these auditions has been, well, *uneven*, but I'm now thinking rich, untapped reservoir, rich, untapped reservoir. And in that spirit, I raise my voice and say, *next*!"

Johnny Slash walked up to the stage. Everyone was watching him as he walked over to the piano, motioned for the piano player to stand up, and then lifted and carried the piano bench from one side of the stage to the other and back again. Then he stood and looked at Mr. Spacek.

Mr. Spacek was rapturous. "This is me, dying again. Open heart surgery time. Chekhov in chinos. You've captured all the alienation and angst of high school."

"Is that good?" asked Johnny.

"Good? It's beyond good. Name the role, and it's yours."

"I don't want to be *in* it. No way," said Johnny. "I want to work backstage. It's darker. Totally different head."

"All right, rain on my parade," said Mr. Spacek. "But I wager I'll have you center stage before the school year is out, Mr. Slash."

Johnny left the stage while Mr. Spacek shuffled through the remaining index cards. "Next!"

Lauren shoved Patty. "You. He means you."

"I'm going to move a piano bench," Patty said. "That's it."

"Wise guy," said Lauren.

Patty slowly walked up on the stage.

Mr. Spacek stared at her. "What we are looking for today," he said, "is pain. And unfortunately, *I* have been the one experiencing most of it. What I'd like to see in you now is P-A-I-N. Wring it out of your skinny little body."

Patty felt a moment of pure terror. Then she took off her glasses and looked at them. Suddenly everything came rushing out. "These?" she said. "These, these are my glasses. I've worn them since I was two.

It's funny—people always feel sorry for little kids who wear glasses. As you get older, people get meaner. But you know, when I was a little kid, I always thought that I'd have this horrible accident and then they'd take off the bandages and I'd be able to see perfectly. Now I know my eyes'll just probably get worse. I hate my glasses."

Mr. Spacek applauded. "You are hearing the sound of two hands clapping. Now if you have only half the honesty in your singing voice. Let me hear it."

Patty looked down at Lauren. She looked at all the kids in the auditorium. She looked at Mr. Spacek. Everyone was waiting.

Patty remembered other waiting faces. She remembered when her mother had driven her around to perform at meetings, at political rallies, at picnics, and once at a bus stop. "What you have is a beautiful voice *and* beautiful, long, although somewhat flyaway hair," her mother always said. Patty had hoped for a longer list. But it was just the voice and the hair, followed by the afterthought "and, of course, massive brains."

Patty tried to sing, but no sound came out. Lauren clutched her hands in prayer.

Patty tried again. This time the sound came. A clear sound, a rich sound.

Mr. Spacek shook his head as if trying to clear it. This must be one of those dreams where things work out just the way you want them to, and then you wake up to reality and try to think of an attention-getting way to commit suicide so you won't depart this earth in obscurity.

But no! He was awake. The voice was honest and real.

Patty sang on. When she was finished, everyone

stood and applauded. Almost everyone. Jennifer said, "Like, there's more pain in melted makeup."

Vinnie was whistling. Lauren was jumping up and down. Mr. Spacek cried, "Brava! Brava!"

Patty stood there and beamed. To herself she said, *I wish to thank my mother, who carted me around from place to place since I was five, who allowed ladies to pinch my cheeks and gush over me and tell me I was too thin to sing in opera but they had this wonderfully fattening recipe—*

"Auditions are over!" said Mr. Spacek.

Muffy Tepperman stood up. "I have a few words to say. Love of communication has been the driving force in my life. I absolutely believe in live theater and in Weemawee High School. Also, I'm thoroughly familiar with appearing in public. And so, people . . ."

Muffy managed to clear the auditorium in four minutes flat.

28

Muffy walked proudly up to the trophy case. She was carrying scripts and a typed cast list. She posted the list, while everyone milled around her. "People—please!"

Vinnie read the list. He seemed pleased with himself. "Alllllllll right!" He danced around. "All right all right. I got it."

Jennifer was glaring at the list. "Like, I thought this was a, you know, musical, like, not a monster movie. Be serious. Patty Greene is, like, the star, and I'm like, head of the, you know, makeup committee? Like, isn't it like, time for a, you know, reality check?"

"Dont' fight it," said Vinnie. "Babe, you're a born beautician and I'm a born leading man."

Jennifer hit Vinnie. He jokingly stepped back and bumped into Patty. He laughed and looked at her chest. "Hey, hey, leading lady, where've you been hiding that big voice of yours?"

Patty was embarrassed. "Vinnie!"

"She was born talented," said Lauren. "It's in her genes."

Jennifer looked at Patty's rear. "Like, no. It's not there either."

Jennifer dragged Vinnie away.

"Don't worry about it," said Lauren. "You just won't thank Jennifer in your Oscar acceptance speech."

Patty was flipping through the script. "Oh, no! Will you look at this? It says here that the drama teacher is smitten by a gawky teen-ager with Coke bottle lenses. I have to wear my glasses onstage!"

"So?"

"So you're the one who's always taking my glasses off for me," said Patty. "Remember?"

"Yes, and now my act is coming back to haunt me," said Lauren. "It isn't nice to throw up a good deed. A silly deed. A *forgettable* deed. Let's just concentrate on the show. Just think, you got the star part Jennifer wanted. She wanted, *you got*! How do you like the sound of that?"

"Like, I like it," said Patty.

"Me, too. And think about it this way. You'll be rehearsing with Vinnie every night. It'll almost be like having a social life."

"Great. Some people have stage mothers. I have a stage best friend."

Johnny Slash crossed in front of Patty and Lauren. He was carrying a cafeteria chair.

"Johnny?" said Patty.

Marshall was following the chair and Johnny. "Shh, don't break his concentration," said Marshall. "He's going to be a scenery changer, and he's practicing."

Johnny looked up. "Do you have anything you want me to carry?" he asked Lauren. "I need the practice."

"There's always Marshall," said Lauren.

"Don't remind him," said Marshall.

Johnny put down the chair and carried Marshall off.

For the next few weeks there was a great deal of activity in the school auditorium. Scenery was built, shabby costumes were tried on, and posters put up around a ticket booth. The posters read, "SEE A SHOW, BUY A SHOE" and 'A CAFETERIA LINE'—ONE SMALL STEP FOR THE WEEMA-WEE DRAMA DEPARTMENT, ONE GIANT STEP FOR GUATEMALA."

The biggest activity centered on the rehearsals. Mr. Spacek was particularly anxious to get a dance scene in the cafeteria just right.

"Now in this scene," he said, "our hero, the Drama Teacher, dances around the cafeteria. It's a metaphor. Wild, isn't it? Okay, places, everyone. Five, six, seven, eight . . ."

The chorus danced and sang:

> How do you make
> Chicken-fried steak?
> How do you eat
> Mystery meat?
> Creamed corn! Catsup as a vegetable.
> Creamed corn! Catsup as a vegetable.
>
> You don't know how I felt
> When I shared your tuna melt.
> I love to sit while you are stuffin'
> Your pretty face with pizza muffin,
> Jell-O squares, and lumpy tapioca.
> Jell-O squares and lumpy tapioca.

Mr. Spacek blew kisses to the dancers. "Okay. Enough of this madness." He clapped his hands. "Vincente, go get Patricia! It's kissy time! Let's get those lights down and lose the vegetables."

Mr. Spacek sent Vinnie to the wings, where Lauren and Patty were waiting. "Y'know," Vinnie said to Patty, "if you're gonna play my student, maybe I should give you some *private* lessons—"

Suddenly Jennifer walked up and started to rub Vinnie's neck. "Like, hi . . ."

"Later, babe. We got to rehearse."

"Well, like, excuuuse, like, me, okay?"

Jennifer rushed off in a huff.

Patty, Lauren, and Vinnie walked to the stage.

Muffy was standing nearby. Lauren whispered to Patty, "This is it. The big kiss."

Mr. Spacek said, "No chattering. Clear the stage for our two lovers. Come on, come on. Now this is the golden moment. The awkward student confesses her love, the love that dare not speak its name. Teacher and student. The ultimate taboo. The same thing happened to me once, only slightly different."

Patty felt nervous. "Well, can't we ask the scenery painters and everybody to leave while we do this?"

Mr. Spacek sighed. "This may come as a hideous shock to your little system, but we're going through this experiment in terror in anticipation of an audience. You know, people in chairs out there, watching?"

Mr. Spacek pointed to Vinnie. "Now, Vinnie, this has to be a big kiss, this is the kiss that says hello . . . and goody-bye."

"No problem," said Vinnie.

"Bless you for understanding," said Mr. Spacek. "Patty, darling, this is the kiss against which you'll measure every other kiss in your life. Okay, have fun. Come on . . . come on . . ."

Jennifer and LaDonna were watching intently behind the curtains. They poked their heads out. They were in each other's way. But they didn't want to miss a thing.

Vinnie started to kiss Patty. Johnny Slash walked between them with a blackboard.

Mr. Spacek called, "Could you do your carrying just a bit later? Or earlier, Mr. Slash? We're trying to rehearse."

"I'm rehearsing carrying this," said Johnny, "so that I can make a totally different scene."

Marshall piped from the sidelines. "A totally different *scene*! A play on words. That's a good one for Johnny Slash. A little appreciation here."

"Mr. Blechtman, if Mr. Slash would care to conk you over the head with his blackboard, I would personally applaud," said Mr. Spacek.

Vinnie started to kiss Patty again. But she giggled nervously. "Sorry," she said. "I just remembered a— a joke."

"Mr. Spacek retired to the wings.

Vinnie tried again.

Mr. Spacek called from the wings, "This is me, waiting."

Vinnie kissed Patty. It almost seemed as if he meant it.

29

Patty and Lauren were walking down the hall toward health and hygiene class. They had to pass between Vinnie and Jennifer.

Vinnie winked at Patty.

"Hey, did I see Vinnie just wink at you?" asked Lauren.

"Yep."

"And right in front of like, you know, Jennifer." Lauren laughed.

"He actually drove by my house this weekend, too," said Patty.

"Vinnie actually drove by your house? How romantic—did you invite him in?"

"Invite him in?" said Patty. "Lauren, my mother may be liberal, but it still takes more than horn honking and wheelies in the driveway to warrant a dinner invitation."

"Let's see," said Lauren, and she suddenly stopped and thought. "He followed you from your locker to homeroom; then he followed you from geometry to the cafeteria—"

"Yes," said Patty. "Vinnie Pasetta is going to make some lucky woman a great Yorkshire terrier."

Jennifer walked up to Patty. She smirked. "Like, I'm making Vinnie be nice to you as a joke, you know? I mean, no way is he, like, serious. Only someone pathetic would believe that Vincent Pasetta likes you. Like, maybe you should, you know, change your, like, name from Patty to, like Patsy, okay?"

Jennifer flounced away.

Patty looked stricken. "I bet she's right, Lauren. Everyone's probably laughing at me behind my back."

Lauren put her hand on Patty's shoulder. "No one's laughing at you. Look, Patty, don't you see what she's doing? Jennifer's threatened by Vinnie's interest in you, so she's trying to make you back off."

Patty brightened. "She is? How do you know?"

All through health and hygiene class Patty thought about what Lauren had said. She found it hard to pay attention to the various diseases she might be carrying. Muffy got into a spirited discussion about Typhoid

Mary. Actually Muffy was having the spirited discussion with herself inasmuch as everybody else in the class thought that Typhoid Mary was the name of a rock group.

The bell rang. It was time for lunch. Patty and Lauren walked to the cafeteria.

In the cafeteria Marshall and Johnny Slash were already eating lunch. In the middle of a bite Johnny stopped, looked down at his Walkman, and tapped it lightly. He waited. Then he tapped it again. And again. Finally he opened it up and pulled out an unraveled cassette. He was in shock.

"I killed it," he moaned.

"Easy, boy, easy," said Marshall. "I'll rewind it for you."

Johnny was horrified. "No! Air touched the music."

Lauren and Patty approached the table with their trays. They were talking about Jennifer. "I think the only difference between you and Jennifer are forty IQ points, a ton of cheap mascara, and three cup sizes," said Lauren. "We'll go downtown this afternoon and get you a complete makeover. Vinnie will never know what hit him."

"Jennifer will hit him," Patty said.

Lauren and Patty sat down with Marshall and Johnny.

"Hi, Marshall, hi, Johnny," said Patty.

"Johnny can't communicate just now," said Marshall. "He's in mourning."

"What happened?" asked Patty.

"Air touched his music," said Marshall.

"Air?" said Lauren. "Sincere condolences, Johnny. Just don't think about it. Time heals. So what are you two doing after school?"

"We're going to check out the sports arena with the dome that collapsed. Wanna come?"

"We'll pass," said Patty.

"Yeah, but we were wondering if you'd drop us off in town. We're going to get a make-over for Patty."

"Don't do it," said Johnny, springing to life. "You're a little skinny, and your hair's weird, but it looks good on you."

"Thanks," said Patty. "I want to learn how to wear makeup, that's all. To bring out the woman in me—"

"When you bring her out, can she stay at my house?" asked Marshall.

Lauren poked Patty. "Patty! Vinnie wants you—over there."

"He doesn't want me," said Patty. "He's just having a muscle spasm."

"Yo, Patty!" called Vinnie.

Elizabeth Barrett Browning, eat your heart out. "He wants me," said Patty as she got up and walked over to Vinnie.

"Patty," said Vinnie, "how would you like, uh, to do something Real Special and Real Meaningful after school?"

Patty frowned. Then she said, "Not before marriage."

Vinnie laughed. "For such a brain, you've really got a great sense of humor. That takes class. But I'm being serious. I think it would be kinda romantic and all if you let me show you, uh, my old paper route."

"What?"

"You know, from when I was a kid. When I was nine, I was a very outrageous paper thrower."

Patty hesitated. "Well, it's a tempting offer, but—I—I'm supposed to go downtown with Lauren and—"

"Hey, this is Vinnie talking. *Vinnie.*"

Patty stood there. What should she do? She had told her friend—her *best* friend—Lauren that she would go downtown to the make-over place with her. Patty asked herself, *Am I the kind of girl who would break a date with her best friend to go out with a guy who's the biggest fox in the freshman class?*

Patty looked at Vinnie. "I see your point," she said. "I don't know what came over me. I'd love, *Like*, to go with you."

Vinnie was feeling cocky. "Three ten. My van. The parking lot. Be there."

Patty walked slowly back to her table. She hated to face Lauren.

Lauren was looking up expectantly. "*Well*?"

"He asked me to see his old paper route," said Patty.

"When a man wants you to share his past, he's serious," said Lauren. "When?"

"Er, today. After school."

"Today? I thought . . ." Lauren's voice trailed off. She sounded let-down.

"I know, Lauren, and I'm sorry," said Patty. "But if the whole reason I was going for a make-over was to attract Vinnie, I don't need it. I already attracted him."

Lauren answered, "Maybe you can do both activities, Patty! First we'll get your makeup; then you can go with Vinnie. That way, when he looks longingly at you, you won't be embarrassed by your bushy eyebrows, no offense."

"Lauren, you're not mad, are you? Me? Vinnie? Popularity? Isn't this what we wanted?"

"I did, but now I don't," Lauren replied.

"Lauren," said Marshall. "You'll go to the sports arena with us, in Johnny's Slashmobile."

"First the dome and then my tape," said Johnny. "Brutal."

"We'll have a little ceremony this afternoon for your tape, Johnny," said Marshall, "if that'll make you feel better. Ladies and gentlemen, we are gathered here to mourn the passing of Johnny Slash's tape. . . . Hey, Lauren, want to go to a funeral?"

"Sure," said Lauren. "I'm in the mood."

Patty looked at Lauren. Lauren looked depressed.

"You don't have to wear black or anything," said Johnny. "I mean, it was *my* tape. Just think of yourself as a friend of the family."

30

Vinnie and Patty were leaning against Vinnie's van.

"This is a nice neighborhood you brought me to, Vinnie," said Patty. "Real suburbia."

"These are my roots," said Vinnie. "This is where Vinnie Pasetta came from. Now you know my whole entire person. A person can be handsome and still have roots, ya know. Now when you see me at Weemawee, you're gonna think *lawns*! You're gonna think *trees*! You're gonna think *roots*!"

Vinnie patted his van. "How'd you like the ride? Kinda like a Holiday Inn with a steering wheel, huh?

And hey, I'm sorry about that picture of Jennifer on the dashboard. It's just there till my uncle gives me his Saint Christopher statue."

Patty stifled a yawn.

Vinnie kept talking. "Now that house over there, I'd aim for the birdbath—especially if there were birds in it. That one with the flamingo on the screen door—I used to get the Yorkie on the head. He'd yak and yak. That house on the left, that's where I hit their kid with the Sunday paper once. He had to get a couple of stitches, but he was okay. Crybaby."

"You have a very interesting past, Vinnie," said Patty, trying even harder not to yawn. Patty had a faraway look in her eyes. She had broken a date with Lauren for a nostalgic look at Vinnie Pasetta's target practice. Johnny Slash's funeral for his cassette tape couldn't be nearly as boring.

Patty wondered if Lauren would ever forgive her.

Lauren, Marshall, and Johnny were sitting in a booth at The Grease. "Aren't you ever going to finish your onion rings, Lauren?" asked Marshall. "I don't want to spend my formative years in The Grease."

Lauren shoveled some onion rings. "I swear, when I'm thirty, these'll be martinis."

Marshall and Johnny stared at her in disbelief.

"Don't look at me that way," said Lauren. "I once had a doctor who warned me about dieting under stress."

"Without Patty I feel like the Three Stooges after Curly died," Marshall said.

Suddenly a shadow fell over their booth. It belonged to Jennifer.

Marshall, imitating a TV commercial, yelled, "*Raid!*"

Jennifer looked down at Lauren. "Like, don't think that us talking is going to be a regular thing or anything, okay?"

"Don't worry, Jennifer," said Marshall. "If anyone sees you here with us, we'll just say we kidnapped you and made you sit down."

Jennifer was busy thinking that over. "Yeah, okay."

Jennifer sat down as Lauren shoved Marshall and Johnny into the corner. Jennifer kept talking to Lauren while she looked at Marshall and Johnny. "These two, like, people," she said, nodding toward them, "are probably fine for you, but this is the first time I haven't had a boyfriend for more than an hour since I was ten. I hate it."

"You still have a boyfriend," said Lauren. "Patty isn't serious about Vinnie."

"Well, like, then what's she doing in his van—homework?"

"For your information, they're not *in* Vinnie's van," said Lauren. "Vinnie wanted to show someone his old paper route—"

"Like, I don't even read newspapers," said Jennifer.

"Details," said Lauren. "Minor, insignificant details."

"Like, I really care what Vinnie did when he was, you know, young, plus like, I read a newspaper once, and it was, you know, disgusting. Like, this black ink got all over my hands and everything. Grossed me out. And like, besides, he never even asked me if I wanted to go."

"Don't let that stand in your way," said Lauren. "He probably felt rejected by your caustic remarks and total lack of interest in him, that's all. I bet he was just scared you'd say no."

Marshall piped up. "Hmm—let's see. Is the word 'no' in Jennifer's vocabulary? I know 'you know' is, and of course, there's our old friend 'like' and 'awesome,' a real biggie—"

Jennifer lunged for Marshall, but Johnny put an arm out between them.

"No more destruction, okay?" said Johnny.

Lauren spoke up. "Jennifer DiNuccio, stand by your man. Go over to his house and ask, beg, plead if you must, but see that paper route if it's the last thing you do."

Jennifer stood up. "Like, I don't get it. Your best friend has got the foxiest guy in school, and you want to break it up. How come?"

"Because," said Lauren, "you and Vinnie belong together. Like Gable and Lombard—"

"Shields and Yarnell," said Marshall.

They stared at Johnny. He panicked. "Spaghetti and peanut butter," he said.

31

It was early morning. Jennifer and Vinnie were leaning against his van. Jennifer was gazing around in awe. "This is, like, a genuine street, like you see, you know, in those TV shows that have trees and, like, lawn mowers and paper boys and people drinking coffee inside the houses. It just freaks me out to see a real TV street in, you know, real life."

"Okay, let me show you how I used to toss the newspaper on this very street," said Vinnie.

Vinnie moved his arm as if he were tossing a big rock.

"Now that house over there, I'd aim for the birdbath—especially if there were birds in it."

Jennifer looked at him dreamily.

Vinnie continued. "That one with the flamingo on the screen door—I used to get the Yorkie on the head. He'd yak and yak. That house on the left, that's where I hit their kid with the Sunday paper once. He had to get a couple of stitches, but he was okay. Crybaby."

Jennifer looked at Vinnie with admiration. "Like, I only wish I'd known you then. A paper, you know, boy."

"Yeah," said Vinnie. "There's a lot you don't know about me."

"I never knew you had, like, emotions and feelings and everything, you know?"

Jennifer kissed Vinnie. "I'll always remember that, like, outside your van, here on this genuine TV street I got to know the genuine, you know, Vinnie Pasetta."

"Yeah, well, there's a lot to take in, so just let it sink in gradually."

32

The next morning at school Lauren was pacing nervously. Patty approached her slowly.

"Hi," said Patty. "You know Marshall was right. I do have star quality."

Lauren was taken aback. "What?"

"Don't you remember his list?" said Patty. "To be a star, you have to be rude, selfish, inconsiderate . . . that's me."

"You're not the only one with star quality," said Lauren. "I was rotten, too. I threw you at Vinnie, and when he caught you, I wanted you back."

"You're right," said Patty. "You were worse than I was."

"Much worse," said Lauren. "I'm the one who sent Jennifer after him."

"You know, all she had to say was 'Like, hi,' and Vinnie forgot all about me."

"I guess the bottom line is cup size trumps IQ," said Lauren.

"And this time friendship trumps popularity," said Patty.

The two friends laughed.

33

It was opening night. Patty couldn't believe that it had finally come. Out there in the audience were her family, friends of her family, and people her mother had corralled, cajoled, and threatened into coming.

Mr. Spacek seemed to have gotten himself together. He was dressed in a designer tuxedo, and he spoke to the opening night audience with poise. He praised everyone in the cast in advance, even those players he was sorry he had allowed in the show.

The audience applauded Mr. Spacek. He bowed and went backstage, where he addressed the cast. "And so always remember that I love each and every one of you, deeply—break your little legs, darlings."

"No way," said Vinnie. "I got a game on Saturday."

Lauren turned to Patty. "Did you hear what Vinnie said? I can't believe he didn't know what 'break a leg' means. Superstitions are the backbone of the theater."

"What are you talking about now?"

"Cool it. Here come Vinnie and Jennifer. Vinnie's got his eye on you."

Vinnie walked up to Patty. "Good luck, doll. You really are a star. I, uh, appreciated your help with, you know, my songs and all—"

Patty shrugged. "Music hath charms—"

Lauren continued dreamily, " '—to soothe the savage breast.' " Suddenly she cringed as Jennifer came up to her.

"Like, I'd really talk if I were you," said Jennifer.

Suddenly the sounds of a pitiful overture were heard. Mr. Spacek ran screaming through the halls.

"Places, children, places, please."

They all took their places. The curtain rose. For Patty the moment was like a dream. She was a singer. She was a star. The auditorium was full. Patty felt . . . popular.

Patty had a strange feeling of ease. She had a sense of gliding through her role. She tried not to think of her mother out in the audience, nudging, whispering, all but getting up and leading a cheer. She tried not to think of all the kids with their eyes so riveted on her that if she made a tiny mistake, it would ripple through the audience. She tried not to think of the glasses she was wearing.

Everything was going well. Mr. Spacek hovered over the players like a benevolent peacock. "Darlings, superb! Darlings, masterful!"

The show was building to the final, climactic moments. It was time for a pivotal scene change. Backstage, Johnny Slash, dressed all in black, was ready to make the change. Marshall, in costume, was standing beside him.

"That's a great outfit, Johnny," said Marshall.

"I like black," said Johnny. "Black is good."

"Yeah, no one'll see you, except for your hair. Why don't you tuck it into a black ski hat or something?"

"I don't wear hats," said Johnny. "Hats are a totally different head."

The scene onstage ended. It was time for Johnny to go out and change the scenery.

"Go, Johnny, go!" said Marshall. "This is your big moment to rearrange the cafeteria."

Johnny rushed onto the darkened stage, carrying a prop and listening to his headphones. Suddenly his tape ran out. "My tape! It's *expired*!" Johnny stopped. He stood there. Then he got busy. He changed his cassette instead of the scenery.

The lights went up. Johnny was standing among big vegetables. Instinctively he whipped on his dark glasses and froze.

The audience applauded. Obviously the man with the dark glasses was meant to be some kind of statue, a monument to man's finding his way through a suddenly illuminated darkness. What this had to do with the plot of *a Cafeteria Line* was not entirely clear, but Patty's mother cheerfully explained to her friends, "Patty told me specifically to watch for this scene."

Marshall ran onstage and led Johnny off, trying to cover him with his jacket as they went. It was now the final scene. Vinnie and Patty were onstage. Vinnie said, "Kid, when the curtain comes up on the second act of your life, always remember: We wrote the lines together."

"Now I know I'll never star alone," said Patty.

"Yeah, but you'll always get top billing," said Vinnie. "And do you know why? Because you earned it."

Patty was gazing soulfully at Vinnie. He returned the look. "You have your whole life to live," he said, "and I've got four more years till I get tenure. There'll be other men, other drama teachers. Always remember: Theater is where you make it."

Vinnie and Patty kissed. Vinnie now had one eye on Jennifer who was standing in the wings. She was slamming her hair dryer menacingly into her hand. Patty was nervously looking to Lauren in the wings for moral support. Lauren was beside herself.

Mr. Spacek was weeping.

Vinnie exited, and Jennifer immediately wiped his mouth off with witch hazel. Patty was now alone on the stage, singing:

> My young life,
> Slow as molasses,
> No boyish passes,
> All because I'm trapped 'neath my glasses.
> Then came you.
>
> Now I love
> A person I can see.
> Oh, I feel so free
> 'Cause the one I'm in love with is me.
> There goes you.
>
> Now I'm standing alone,
> But I'm not alone—I'm with me.
> Now that you've touched my life with love
> I can seeeeeee.

Everyone was applauding. She was a hit.

34

The show was over. It was a big hit. There were several curtain calls. Patty and Vinnie got the biggest ovations, followed closely by Johnny Slash. Mr. Spacek was beaming. He was glad he hadn't tried to become a clothing designer after all. But he wasn't terribly glad. Perhaps in another fifty or sixty years he would direct another student musical.

Everyone was celebrating. Vinnie, with his arm around Patty, was talking to Mr. Spacek. "So, like, I'm thinking maybe the Spring Musical could be something like *A Newspaper Route* with songs—"

Lauren pulled Patty away.

"Hey, I liked where I was," said Patty.

"But I have to talk!" said Lauren. "We did it! I almost died when Vinnie was kissing you. It was extremely passionate. He never did it like that during rehearsals."

Patty turned coy. "Yes, he did."

"He did?"

"But it didn't mean anything . . . to him. Besides, he was thinking of Jennifer while he was kissing me."

"How do you know?" asked Lauren.

"Afterward he told me it was the first time in a year that he kissed something that didn't taste like strawberry lip gloss."

"Well, speaking of the gloss taster, here he comes," said Lauren.

Vinnie rushed up to Patty. "How about an encore?" said Vinnie, giving Patty a hug and a kiss.

Patty and Lauren exchanged ecstatic looks.

Lauren swooned. "Art imitates life."

Marshall walked up. "I can imitate E.T.," he said.

Jennifer was standing there, glaring at Patty. "Like, I think maybe somebody's gonna imitate a, you know, dead girl real soon."

35

Patty, Marshall, and Johnny were standing in the hallway. Lauren rushed up, waving a newspaper. "I can't believe you didn't see this. Our first review. Listen," said Lauren. " 'The most exciting stage duo this reviewer has ever seen, Patty Greene and Vincent Pasetta, lit up the auditorium, and we can only hope that director Jon-Michael Spacek will give us more plays starring this glittering couple.' "

Lauren grabbed Patty. "Oh, Patty!"

"Let me see that," said Patty. Patty read the review. She had never seen anything so beautiful in print.

Johnny gazed into space. "They didn't even mention my name. I must have been terrible. Why didn't anyone tell me I was terrible?"

"They were stunned by your performance, Johnny," said Marshall. "Your moment on the cafeteria table was too much for their meager supply of adjectives. The best they could have come up with was 'riveting,' but that hardly begins to describe it."

Johnny went on. "Once I read that a scenery changer carried a prop adroitly. *Adroitly.* I like that. That sounds like me. I would have been happy with 'adroitly.' "

"Next edition, Johnny," said Marshall.

Patty reread the review. Then she said, "I wonder why we didn't get our paper this morning. I want my mother to see this."

"Yeah, we didn't get ours either," said Marshall.

"We never get one," said Johnny.

Patty and Lauren started to walk down the hall. As they turned a corner, they saw Vinnie in a plastic beautician's cape. He was sitting patiently while Jennifer cut his hair.

"Like, I don't know what you did to him, Patty, but like, it really raunched out his hair."

Jennifer took a huge snip and threw the hair on the ground. The ground was covered with newspapers. The headlines of all the newspapers read A CAFETERIA LINE BOWS AT WEEMAWEE.

Patty and Lauren laughed and walked on.

36

Patty's telephone didn't stop ringing. "Congratulations, congratulations, congratulations," said Patty. "The word is singing in my ears. And I do like that song!"

"Don't get a swelled head," Lauren warned.

"Why not?" said Patty. "It's a lot better than the other kind."

Patty started to count the telephone calls. "Number eighteen," she said to herself as she ran to pick up the receiver. She hoped this would be a short one. She had an appointment with Lauren.

"Hi, this is Patty Greene speaking," she answered. It was her new way of answering the telephone. She hoped it reflected her new confidence.

"Patty?"

Patty couldn't place the voice. It wasn't familiar and it wasn't unfamiliar. She did know it from somewhere. Probably it belonged to someone from her past. Before she was a star.

"This is Wayne. Wayne Feiger, in case you know some other Waynes."

Wayne? Why was he calling her? Wasn't he supposed to go down the road of life with Muffy Tepperman?

"I'm calling with good news," said Wayne.

"How absolutely terrific," said Patty. "That means you and Muffy are going steady or something?"

Please be going steady with Muffy Tepperman! Patty would have felt better if she had seem them together at least once. Just *once*.

"My good news," said Wayne, "is that I'm new and improved. Like a product that needed some re-alignment or jazzing up. I finally woke up and realized I had one thing wrong with me. Know what that was?"

"Can't begin to guess," said Patty.

"Well, I hate to say it, but it was my mother. It was a psychological thing like the umbilical cord between us not being broken. Well, I broke it. I'm weaned. Completely. I stay out late nights, and I don't even tell my mother where I'm going. I don't report to her when I come home from school. I don't allow her to polish and wax my keys anymore. I'm your total rebel."

"How's your mother taking it?"

"Not well at all. She took away my blow dryer, my allowance, and all my green sweaters. She's threatening to melt my keys and sell them for scrap. Am I boring you?"

"Not any more than usual. No, I mean, my life is usually boring."

"Well, good. That gives me hope. Because guess what I'm going to do?"

"What?"

"I'm going to ask you out and *not tell my mother!*"

"Oh."

"It's all on the sly. I'm going to pick you up, take you out, and not even let her know. So how about now?"

"I've got an appointment with Lauren."

"Right after that?"

"It might take all afternoon."

"Then how about tonight?"

"Well, I think I'm busy."

"That uses up today," said Wayne. "So how about tomorrow?"

"You're kind of persistent," said Patty.

"Good. You're supposed to notice that," said Wayne. "I never was before. It's macho, isn't it? Before this, the only one in the family who was macho was my mother."

"I noticed."

"So how about it? Tomorrow afternoon? My place."

"*Your* place?"

"My mother has her bridge club tomorrow afternoon." Wayne chuckled. "Across town. Clear across town."

"Uh, can I call you back, Wayne?"

"When? Name a time."

"I can't."

" 'Can't' isn't in my vocabulary anymore," said Wayne. "So why should it be in yours? Simply stated, I'm emancipated."

Patty was silent.

"If you stick with me," said Wayne, "I'll convert you. You'll never have to tell your mother anything again. I want you to think about that, and *I'll* call *you* back."

"Oh, good. No, not good. Uh, gotta go," said Patty.

"The next call you get will be from . . . Tiger Feiger," said Wayne.

"*Tiger* Feiger?"

37

"You won't regret this," said Lauren as she and Patty walked into Marjorie's Make-over Boutique Franchise.

"But it looks so intimidating," said Patty.

"It's supposed to," said Lauren. "Anybody who wants to be made over is a natural candidate for intimidation. I think they'll do more for you if you cower a little."

A woman with frizzy hair approached them.

"We're your three o'clock appointment," said Lauren. "That is, my friend here is. She had to break her previous appointment because of a conflicting appointment in regard to a newspaper situation." Lauren smiled brightly.

The woman studied Patty. "Heavens, what shall we attack first? The hair, the eyebrows, the burgeoning blotch?"

"Hey, just a minute," said Lauren. "You're talking about my best friend."

"Now don't be impatient," said the woman. "You'll get your turn. Did you know there's a growing trend toward *colored* braces? The idea is to treat braces like a fashion accessory rather than an appliance. It's the same thinking that went into turning your basic bland utilitarian refrigerator, stove, washing machine, and dryer into a veritable rainbow of colors—mauve, tan, charcoal, lilac, robin's-egg blue—"

"My friend looks great in her bland utilitarian braces," said Patty.

"Don't get self-protective," said the woman. "There's no place for vanity in a place like this."

"There isn't?" said Lauren.

"No, this is a place where we face our flaws, where we deal with them."

"Well, my friend is flawless," said Lauren.

"Then why did you make an appointment for her?"

Lauren turned to Patty. "Why did I?"

Patty shrugged.

"We have a memory loss," said Lauren. "Does Marjorie have a franchise for that?"

"If you wait a moment, I'll look it up," said the woman. And she turned away.

"One, two, three, *Retreat*!" said Lauren. She and Patty ran out of the boutique.

They linked arms and walked down the street toward The Grease.

"Maybe we just blew our chance to be popular," said Patty.

"Don't you feel popular? You're a star."

"Well, aren't you the one who said stardom doesn't last?"

"Yeah, but it should be good for another five days or so. And my being your best friend makes me popular by connection or something."

"Okay, so let's enjoy our popularity for the next five days," said Patty.

"Yeah, when we lose it, we'll just pick ourselves up and start working on it all over again," said Lauren.

They walked into The Grease. They looked around. Vinnie, Jennifer, and LaDonna were squeezed into a booth.

Patty turned to Lauren. "Are we sure we *want* to be popular with *them*? Sometimes I think Weemawee High is, well, insane. What do you think?"

"It's a marginally insane school," said Lauren. "No doubt about it."

Just then Marshall called to them from the booth where he was sitting with Johnny.

"We're being summoned," said Patty. "Should we or shouldn't we?"

"We might as well sit where there's room," said Lauren. "Besides, we've got the rest of the year to try out my new popularity plan."

"What new plan?" asked Patty.

"I'll think about that tomorrow," Lauren replied.

The two friends laughed as they walked over to Johnny and Marshall's booth.